ANNIHILATION

A DONATELLA NOVEL

DEMETRIUS JACKSON

PROLOGUE

Donatella ran, arms pumping, lungs burning. Her mind told her, *you still have time*; however, her heart warned her, *you're already too late.*

She blocked out the competing judgements in her head and instead focused on the fury emanating deep within her core. She should have seen this inevitable outcome; she should have prevented it.

Moving at top speed, she conquered the last corner to witness black smoke billowing skyward. This was the first sign that her heart was correct and it tugged at her emotions as she ran harder. A building that was normally present in the landscape was ominously missing.

She wordlessly internalized a prayer and outwardly a tear began to materialize. She distantly heard a horn blaring from her left as she ran through the intersection. The smoke previously in the background now gave a glimpse of its origin. The normally smooth concrete structure of the building lay crumbled and tangled with its typically unseen metal skeleton.

Upon later reflection she would recall hearing the

screams and pleas amidst the rubble, but in this moment, she could only hear her failure. She could feel her mind beginning to side with her heart as despair began to settle.

Fire trucks and EMS crews raced past her seeking the reason for the frantic calls.

Donatella knew the reason and she knew the arbiter of this heinous act.

Arriving at the scene of what was once a five-story building, she now saw smoke, rubble, ash, and destruction. Resigned to the fact that she had failed those she had sworn to protect, her mind and heart agreed at last.

With one final look, her eyes took in the destruction, while her mind and heart became resolute in their agreement - *Terri Buckley would not live to see the sun rise another day*.

Donatella sat in the highbacked, counter-height chair with her eyes transfixed on the steam emanating from the simmering dish. The offbeat rhythm of her heart pulsated against her ear drums. A bead of sweat began to trickle down the crease of her back tracing her spine. Although she was breathing, she felt like she was suffocating.

A gentle hand caressed her tensing shoulder, "Are you ok?" came the concerned voice of Jasmyn Thompson breaking her trance.

She blinked three times in rapid succession, clearing her eyes and her mind. "Yes, I'm fine," Donatella responded in her familiar southern drawl.

She could feel the concern register on Jasmyn's face without even turning to face the woman.

Jasmyn, a registered nurse, noted the signs of PTSD flowing through her friend. She casually walked over to the stove, reduced the flame on the burner, and placed a lid on the pot.

The ordeal that played out at the Cleveland Museum of Art just four months prior left Donatella hospitalized and clinging to life. Jasmyn remained silent on the issue and the ordeal, but she knew the experience weighed heavy on the special agent.

"Dinner will be ready in 15 minutes. I have everything handled in here. Why don't you go spend some time with Sebastian? He loves seeing his godmother."

As if in a trance, Donatella stood from the chair and padded toward the family room. The erect posture and graceful stride synonymous to the special agent was now lost. She now moved with sloped shoulders and a perceptible shuffling of her feet.

Marcellous, who sat with Sebastian cradled in his arm feeding him a bottle, looked up at the approaching figure. "Hey Donatella, he's just finishing up his bottle and should be ready for a good burping. Would you like to do the honors?"

Before she could answer, she felt the cell phone vibrate in her pocket. She eyed the screen, *private number.*

"Hello," she said listlessly.

"As I live and breathe, I cannot for the life of me understand how you're still alive," said the voice on the phone. Marcellous watched as Donatella's dull eyes sharpened and her back stiffened.

"And to think, you are prepared to sit down with the Thompsons for a nice family dinner. By the way, I love what they've done with the place."

Frantically, Donatella's head whipped around the room peering into every corner. With urgency in her gait, she began walking through the house with her phone plastered to her face.

Marcellous, witnessing the change in demeanor, looked over at his wife. Catching her eye, he quickly jerked his head in the direction of the special agent. He still had the baby in his arms and was compromised to make any sudden movement. Jasmyn caught his signal and began after her.

"No need to go rushing around the house like a mad woman," the voice teased from the other end. "Rest assured I'm nowhere near you or your precious friends." The last word rolled from her tongue with a hint of disdain.

The edge in her voice returned, "What do you want, Buckley?" She began climbing the stairs, determined to ensure that they were alone.

"Well, Special Agent Dabria, to my dismay ending your existence hasn't been the trivial task I assumed it would be. And to be quite frank, it's beginning to piss me off. You're like a damn cat with nine lives."

"But," she said taking a deep, exaggerated breath, "if I'm being honest with myself, it's all my fault. I allowed my fostered hatred of you to blind me. In our previous encounters, I missed the inconceivable outs you could manufacture."

Dabria entered into the baby's room, *empty*.

"I wasted so much time trying to affect you through others that I was oblivious to the solution."

Donatella pushed her way down the hallway looking into the first guest room. She peered into the room, *empty*.

"I need to focus all my energy, my efforts, squarely on you."

Donatella could hear the foot falls of someone behind

her and by the pace she knew it was Jasmyn. She blocked it from her mind and proceeded to the master suite.

Inside the suite, she could hear a faint sound originating from outside the bedroom window. She hurried over to the window, pulled back the curtains, and stood face-to-face with an XactSense Titan drone. Affixed just below the camera was Terri Buckley's Bureau picture.

"Damn girl, you look more haggard than I remembered. Appears you're not getting enough rest. You certainly must sleep more, but I digress."

Donatella, familiar with the specs for this particular drone, knew it had a 10-mile operating range. Even if she rushed down the stairs to her car, Terri would be long gone before she could locate her.

"You and I are going to play a little game since I know how much you enjoy our games. This game will be slightly different than our last one."

The veiled reference was to the trap that Buckley set at the Orbitz Technology Campus. During this particular "game" Donatella was faced with saving the life of her goddaughter, Bree, or saving the life of Sal Grandson, a journalist she had met a few weeks prior.

The trap was intended to take the life of both Donatella and Bree; however, Special Agent Dabria was able to thwart the plan, saving both Bree and Grandson. Donatella still wore battle scars from the encounter and vowed Buckley would pay for the role she played in the abduction.

"To prove what a good sport I am, I will leave your family and your friends out of this round. Case and point, I know where the Thompsons and their new bundle of joy reside. I even know where you've tucked away those you attempted to hide from me."

Rage flashed behind Donatella's eyes as she gripped the cell phone tighter. "That's right, I know Bree and her family are stashed away in Illinois. I must say, the Bureau has gotten sloppy with the witness protection protocols since my departure. That's another thing you should look into."

Donatella could feel Jasmyn's presence looming over her shoulder. "If you –"

"If I what!" Buckley's voice boomed through the handset. "I could have arranged a car accident to wipe out that entire family and no one would have been the wiser. But like I said," her voice returning to its patronizing tone, "going after them is not serving the purpose I want – I need."

"Then spit it out! What do you want?!"

"It's simple. I have some scores to settle, and some fun to be had. In a couple of weeks, I will send you a clue as to what target I have in mind. If you are as good as you claim to be, you'll be able to save those in peril; however, should you fail, they will meet their demise. Rest assured, these are targets I have selected for my own personal reasons."

"You're a despicable monster," Donatella screamed into the phone.

"And you, Donatella, are a self-righteous, self-serving, goody two shoes bitch!

Now," Terri said pulling back her rage once again, "where was I?"

"Once I've had my fun in this city, you and I will square off one-on-one. This cat and mouse game of ours will come to an end. Once and for all we will see who's the better woman. Either you will die, or I will die."

The phone went silent, and Terri's words echoed inside Donatella's mind. "With that said, I suggest you get some rest over the next few weeks. You'll need it."

Donatella stood stark still staring out of the window as the drone began maneuvering away. Jasmyn, who stood in the shadows during the exchange, took a few steps in the direction of Donatella. Fearing she knew the response before the question left her lips, she inquired anyway.

"Is everything alright, Donatella?"

She cautiously walked around so that she could face the agent. Both of her eyes were closed and her breathing had become slow and measured.

Jasmyn began to wonder if she should say something more, but instead she stood there; looking, staring, watching. She could sense the demeanor shifting within the woman standing motionless in front of her.

When Donatella opened her eyes, her hazelnut brown eyes, the intensity, determination, and resolve had been returned to them. Jasmyn, on several occasions, witnessed the reactions others had when they were on the receiving end of Donatella's piercing glare. Now, as the special agent focused in her direction, those eyes burning a hole through her soul, she had firsthand knowledge of what those others had experienced.

With measured, haunting words she said, "Terri Buckley is back in town. And this time, make no mistake, she will be held responsible for all the mayhem she has caused."

Donatella spun and begun to make her way to the door. "I'll need to pass on our dinner, it seems that there is some prep I need to do before our next encounter."

The long, elegant stride was back in her steps and, self-ishly, Jasmyn thought, *go kick her ass!*

IN A DARK ROOM, adjacent to the master suite at 300 Calgary Lane, Donatella sat in the middle of the floor entrenched in meditation. She concentrated on the moment that her aunt broke the news to her concerning her parents.

A KNOCK CAME from the partially opened door, "Sweetheart," the tremulous voice started. "Do you mind if I come in?"

When she turned to face her Aunt Susan, she observed the dried streaks of tears, the puffy nose, and the bloodshot eyes.

Not waiting to receive a formal invitation, Susan walks into the room and sits next to her on the bed. "I'm afraid I have some," her voice trembled and cracked as she fought back the tears. Composing herself she continued, "I have some terrible news."

Susan did what she could to look her niece in the eyes. She did what she could to be the strong one, but she was failing. Donatella's young, naive eyes couldn't fathom that her world was about to be forever changed.

"There's no easy way to say this, but," she paused again knowing the next words from her mouth were going to be devastating. "Last night after your parents boarded the yacht, there was an explosion."

"An explosion," inquired her young, smooth mellow voice. "What kind of explosion?"

"Sweetheart," she said again, running her fingers through her niece's jet-black hair. "The yacht exploded shortly after your parents boarded the vessel. Your mom, your dad, and everyone else onboard the yacht was instantly killed."

Donatella felt the room contract and expand as dizziness set in. Her hazelnut brown eyes filled with tears and an unrelenting pain grabbed at her chest. She found that she could not breath because her mind quit processing the oxygen entering her body.

"Donatella," the distant disembodied voice called. Her aunt's image turned into translucent colors of red, blue, purple, and orange as she looked at her through tear-filled eyes.

Her breathing became more labored, the pain in her chest grew stronger, the room spun faster. And then she was out. Her body dropped lifelessly into the arms of her grieving aunt.

STILL DEEP IN MEDITATION, Donatella shifted to a training session with Master Yoshida, her Krav Maga sensei.

"STAND!" came the stern voice of Master Yoshida. It was the third time during this sparring session that she pulled herself from the mat.

Picking her aching bones up from the canvas, she stood once again.

"Donatella," he said in his fatherly tone. "Why is it that I continue to defeat you?" "Because you're better than me," came the quick response.

He waved his hand in dismissal. "Nonsense girl. Am I stronger than you? Faster than you?"

"No, sensei."

"I continue to defeat you because I use this," he said, tapping her forehead with his forefinger. "Strength and speed are assets in combat; however, if you can anticipate your attacker's next move, you can formulate your next move."

The wheels began to churn in her mind.

"You have mastered the physical disciplines necessary to be a great martial artist, but now it's time to sharpen your mental aptitude."

She nodded her head in affirmation, "Yes, sensei."

The fatherly tone and verbal lesson were over. He took his position and, with his familiarly stern voice, said, "Again!"

She slowly opened her eyes while simultaneously inhaling a deep breath. Recalling the death of her parents always saddened her, but it also gave her the strength she needed to focus. She lived her life to one day bring their killers to justice, even if it was her personal brand of justice.

Donatella's phone vibrated revealing a message from her superior, SSA John Brewer. *Please stop by the office at your earliest convenience.*

She stood from her seated position, placed the phone in her pocket and headed to the door.

2

V eronica King sat at the oversized dinette in her morning room sipping on a cooling cup of coffee. Through the double-pane windows located on the east side of the house, the first rays of sunlight illuminated the otherwise dark space.

Her mind toiled tirelessly reliving the decisions she'd made over the last several months. Decisions that when she closed her eyes, day or night, still haunted her. Never one to be meek, she went after what she wanted. As of late, she felt her life was controlling her more than she was controlling it.

Her life had been in complete chaos from the moment Terri Buckley stepped into her office at Global Insights Security. She conceded the fact that she was now at the helm of the company where she'd spent her entire career, but at what price.

Her late husband, Kyle, was exposed for trying to run off with their daughter and his mistress, something she felt gratified in resolving. Her peers, colleagues, and friends met an untimely and gruesome end which served as the catalyst to her bouts of insomnia. And then there was The Syndicate.

From everything she was able to gather on this criminal organization, they were everywhere and nowhere. They were hidden in plain sight. They managed to fly under the radar while causing mass destruction.

When the GIS Board of Directors were eliminated, the Syndicate provided recommendations for who should fill the vacant seats. Veronica felt that most, if not all, had direct ties to the organization.

To make matters worse, as if they could get any worse, she was now being forced to work for them or they threatened that her daughter, Gina, would be placed in harm's way.

She took another sip of her coffee as more daylight crept into the morning room.

During the dark hours of the night while her insomnia raged, Veronica decided on a plan of action. In the preceding months when she realized her fate was sealed, she decided she would not play the victim. She would hitch her wagon to The Syndicate, if for nothing else, to ensure the safety of her daughter.

But last night, a surge awakened in her. Clarity rang as she looked at the clock that mocked her, *3:03 a.m.* Only 10 minutes since the last time she had looked at it. Just as she had climbed the ranks within GIS she could do so, and would do so, within The Syndicate.

For the next two hours, she mentally devised a plan of action. During the first of several intrusions into her home, she met via video conference with three members of the organization, one of which she was sure now sat on her board at GIS.

Although their silhouettes were the only visible images, she deduced the person in charge. It was the woman who sat in the middle and directed the conversation. In her hastily thrown together, sleep-deprived plan, she needed to learn everything she could about this organization. And before throwing back the covers and climbing from the bed she thought, *I need to find this woman.*

Every company had staff and every company had executives. For Veronica King, being part of the staff was not in the cards. If she would be forced into servitude for this organization, she needed to wield more power.

She would not be an errand boy, or a worker bee. When she sentenced her colleagues to death, she also acted as their executioner. When she saw to it that her husband would never be heard from again, she felt it. She felt the power and absolute decision making.

As she stood in the shower, the relentless hot water pounding on her neck and back, she mulled over her options to get to the shadowy figure. She could simply hash out a conversation with Buckley, but that would not work. Buckley, she thought with a sardonic grin, was a worker bee, an order taker.

No, she needed someone further up the food chain. She needed someone who already worked closely with her prey. She needed Lydia Brooks, the other woman who appeared on the video conference during their first meeting. The woman who was now sitting on her board of directors.

While this was a hunch, she felt confident in her assertion. Lydia would be able to point her in the right direction and today she would start down that path.

King took one more sip of her coffee and glared down at

her Movado Swiss Bold black, ceramic watch. It was now a quarter past seven, *no time like the present,* she thought.

She picked up her cell phone from the table, used facial recognition to gain access and dialed the number. After two rings a voice on the other end answered.

"Good morning, Ms. Brooks," King said in her most disarming voice. "We need to meet. Let's meet me at the country club at nine. We have some business to discuss."

3

I nside the oversized, dank elevator the music droned on in the background while Donatella pondered the reason why she was summoned. This was her first visit to the FBI building at 3700 Wicker St. since she returned from the Cleveland Museum of Art case. She spoke to Brewer on several occasions during her time away but visiting her superior in person today left her conflicted.

At this point in her career, Brewer was lenient with her caseload and managed with a hands-off approach. The manner in which Donatella closed cases were at times unorthodox, nonetheless her close rate was the highest in the Charlotte field office.

However, her last two cases produced a higher than acceptable body count. To make matters worse, she had not apprehended her former partner, Terri Buckley. She assumed that the leniency she enjoyed from Brewer over the years would be tightening as a result of her recent cases and she couldn't fault him for that. She prayed he wouldn't reel her in completely because she still needed to contend with The Syndicate.

The elevator doors opened on well-oiled rollers producing minimum sound. For the moment, everyone's noses were buried in their tasks overlooking her arrival on the floor. However, once she strode to Brewer's office, located in the corner of the expansive open- floor concept, a few heads lifted and necks craned. Instantaneously, muffed conversation began cascading from several locations on the floor. Dignifying the spur-of-the-moment hushed discussions with a glance was unnecessary, furthermore she would not give them the satisfaction.

She heard the watercooler gossip around the office about her inability to apprehend Buckley. Moreover, many of her peers felt the former agent was getting the best of her with each encounter. Donatella heard the whispers and for some, seeing Terri best her gave them a demented sense of pleasure.

Wiping the negativity, and her peers, from her mind she tapped on Brewer's partially open door. He slowly looked up from the case he was analyzing when his eyes met hers.

His eyes were exhausted, dull, and lacked the intensity she always attributed to him. However, his face was eager, determined, formidable. She wasn't certain what to make of the conflicting body signals and why he summoned her to the office today.

"Donatella," he said with a warm inviting smile. "Come in and take a seat."

She walked across the room searching out the visitor's chair when she realized the office hadn't changed much from her first visit.

Brewer stood extending his hand in greeting, "Special Agent Dabria, thank you for coming in so soon."

"Your message seemed urgent," she said in her honeyed voice as she sat crossing her legs.

"My apologies," he responded taking his seat. "There is no cause for alarm. In fact, it's a time of celebration."

She raised an inquisitive eyebrow.

"When I took the reins of the Charlotte field office, I felt I had something to prove. I desired a challenge, a fresh beginning. Nancy still gives me shit because I agreed to the job without first talking it through with her. I knew she wanted me to ease into retirement, but I couldn't. I couldn't leave with so much still undone."

He shifted in his chair; eyes heavy with water as he grabbed the picture from his desk – the only personal item on the surface. "Even though she was furious that I decided to take this post, she stuck with me," he said turning the picture to face her.

For years Donatella wondered about the picture in the frame, but she refused to invade his personal space.

In the frame, a younger Brewer held the hand of Mrs. Brewer in front of a beach sunset. She wore an elegant, white knee-length dress while he sported a white linen, two-piece suit with his shirt open at the collar. They each wore a beaming smile on their faces while gazing into each other's eyes.

"That picture is from 10 years ago. Nancy wanted to renew our vows in a beach ceremony. Initially, I was apprehensive about the ceremony because we were already married and I didn't see the wisdom in doing it again. However, on the day of the renewal, butterflies churned in my stomach, much like on our original wedding day. I felt like I was marrying her for the first time all over again."

A broad smile began to creep along his features as he spoke.

"For the last several months, feelings of selfishness and guilt have eaten away at me.

I knew she wanted me to ease into retirement, but I wanted a sense of adventure that I didn't experience in my previous field office. Not clearing the move with her continues to give me an uneasy feeling."

Taking the picture back from Donatella, he looked at it one more time prior to returning it to its designated spot.

"Nancy never forgot what happened to my previous partner," he subconsciously looked down to the drawer where he kept her shield. "She worries that the dangers of the job may one day cost me my life as well. I see a visible sigh of relief each day I return home from the office."

Brewer again focused his attention on Donatella. "I think it's time I put an end to her worry. What I guess I'm saying is, I have decided to retire."

The smile that had been creeping over his features was now plastered across his face.

"I know this may come as a bit of a surprise, but now is the right time. I wanted you to hear it from me, directly, prior to the announcement that will go out later today.

Donatella," he said in his fatherly voice, "You helped me to right a wrong early on in your career and it's something I have never forgotten. While I hoped we could bring closure to the demons that are haunting you, I'm afraid to say I will not see you reach that finish line."

Early in her career, Donatella was able to track down the

person responsible for the death of Brewer's partner. The individual in question also worked for The Syndicate, and Donatella saw this as an opportunity to obtain answers in the hunt for her parents' killers.

Donatella returned a genuine smile, "Congratulations. What are your plans during retirement?"

"I promised Nancy a tour of Europe a few years ago, so I better make good on that. Furthermore, I look forward to growing old while we sit on the porch enjoying our new rocking chairs."

Brewer leaned forward in his chair lowering his voice, "I was able to provide input into the selection of my successor, but my recommendation is not final. Regardless of the next person to sit in this seat, you may be reeled in more than I have done to this point.

My only greatest regret is that Terri Buckley is still on the streets."

The mention of Buckley's name caused Donatella to shift in her chair.

"I expected to apprehend her before I walked out of this building for the last time, but I doubt that will be the case. Nonetheless, I don't want you to give up. I want you to find her, I want you to locate the head of The Syndicate, and I want you to take them down."

Donatella began to speak when Brewer stayed her with a raised hand. "You have everything it takes to be an amazing agent, but you continue to fight this battle on Buckley's terms. It rips me apart to witness how ruthless she has become, and her lack of empathy makes her extremely dangerous. It's time that you reevaluate your approach.

Buckley is constantly one step ahead of you. You need to

find a way to be one step ahead of her or it could mean disaster."

Brewer leaned back in his chair, "But enough of that talk. I hear rumors that the brass is going all out to celebrate my retirement; I hope that you will be there."

"Absolutely. I wouldn't miss it for anything."

The pair stood from their chairs concluding the meeting. On the way back to the elevator, the conversation with Brewer replayed in her mind. She agreed that she needed to get a step ahead of Terri, but after what transpired at the Thompson's house, she felt she was already a step behind.

4

An impatient silence cascaded throughout the dilapidated commercial building. The occupants consisted of the most ruthless criminals in, and around the city. Each one eyeballed the others with skepticism while pondering why they were summoned here today.

Francene Little, a tall, slender black woman with short, cropped blonde hair, was the newest crook within the bunch. She had the innate ability to infiltrate impenetrable locations without being seen, and without leaving a trace.

Most of her handy work took place within residential dwellings; however, consensus has her knocking off a safe at Wells Fargo as her last job. A job that took place during the middle of the day with no video footage of her being on the premises.

"Any idea why we're here?" she asked of the only other woman in the room that was standing next to her. "I mean, I received the invitation same as everyone else. 'Ready to make a name for yourself while earning $100K for a few weeks of work?' Wonder what it could be. At present I don't need the money, but I'm always up for honing my skills."

"Who the hell called this ragtag group together?" boomed a voice from outside the room where the group had assembled. Walter Vann, a drug-smuggling, child-trafficking menace, ambled sideway through the door's opening. His 6-foot 5-inch height allowed him to look over the crowd where only a few in attendance could look him squarely in the eye without craning their necks.

The corners of his mouth began to curl when he noticed the two women standing off to the side. He began walking in their direction, eyes fixated on Francene. The crowd parted to avoid impeding his progress.

"Well, I don't know the reason that we have been asked here, but you can keep the money if I can have a few weeks with this one." He licked his lips while giving her the once over. "Yes, you would do well. Quite well indeed."

He extended his gnarled hand to caress the side of her face, but Francene deftly avoided his touch while simultaneously extending a blade against his neck.

"Walter," she said, applying additional pressure against his skin. "If you don't want me to paint the concrete with your hot blood, I suggest you keep your hands away from me."

He dropped his hand back to his side, "Bitch!" he uttered under his breath as he walked away.

Terri Buckley, who was standing next to Francene during this exchange, couldn't resist a smirk. With the appearance of Walter Vann, the entire party was present, and it was time to get started.

She activated the wireless mic before taking her place on

the stage. "Thank you for coming," she said as the group turned to face her.

"Great, now the other one has something to say," Vann said, turning his nose up at the appearance of Buckley.

Before this is over, I will have to dispose of him permanently, she thought before continuing. She pulled out her cell phone and spoke, "You're all wondering why you are here today, but before we get into any specifics, we need to discuss some ground rules."

She pushed a couple of buttons on her phone, "The first, and most important rule, while you are working on this assignment is that your silence is not only expected but it is required. Anyone who breaks this rule will be not live to tell anyone else."

Whispers started within the group, but as they studied her demeanor, they realized the gravity in her words.

"As a sign of good faith, a deposit has been made into your personal accounts. However, that deposit comes with the condition that you agree to rule number one. Please, go ahead and check your phones."

Each of them retrieved their phones from their pocket to see a notification waiting on their home screens. Francene utilized the facial recognition feature to unlock her phone. The notification was from her bank, Wells Fargo, alerting her of a deposit of $25,000 applied to her account.

Several thoughts swirled through her mind at the same time. *Who is this woman? How did they gain access to my account? What is this job?* Her phone vibrated in her hand and a message was displayed on the screen.

.   .   .

IF YOU ACCEPT the condition that has been laid out for you, please click accept. If you do not accept the condition, click decline. Please note, if you select decline, you will be asked to leave the premises immediately and the $25,000 will be removed from your account.

"WHAT THE HELL IS THIS, and just who in the hell do you think you are?" Vann blurted. "I assume you can read, Mr. Vann, otherwise you would not be here today. Unless," she said with a sardonic grin, "someone read the invitation to you."

Rage overcame his facial features, but Buckley continued, "It's simple. If you decide to stay, you are expected to click accept. At which point the money will be yours, and you are expected to abide by the rule of silence. If you break the rule, death will be consequence."

"And if we decline?" came another voice from the back.

"Then when you click decline, the money will be extracted from your account and you will be asked to leave. No harm, no foul."

Before Buckley could complete her explanation, Francene pressed the accept button. She was in no matter what. She was looking for some excitement, and this appeared to be right up her alley.

Slowly but surely the others in attendance began casting their votes. By her count, only one person had declined the invitation to this exclusive group, but Vann was still pondering his decision.

After staring down Buckley for a few minutes he clicked on the accept button. She looked down at her phone realizing that all votes had been casted.

"Good, let's get started!"

"Wait just one minute," thundered Walter from within the crowd. "While I appreciate the advance payment, I demand we speak to the man in charge. I appreciate him trotting your sexy ass out here as eye candy, but I will not be taking any additional directions from you."

Buckley decided that enough was enough. She stepped down from her elevated surface, eyeing Walter with each step. She inadvertently bumped into Francene once she reached the bottom step.

The crowd began to part, similar to how they did for Vann, as she made her way to him. "You're accustomed to women serving you I see," she dropped to her knees directly in front of him.

A deprecating smile came over his face, but before he could speak, she struck him with speed and force connecting with his sciatic nerve in his right leg, followed by his left.

Vann felt an intense, shooting pain followed by a numbing sensation creeping down his leg. Within a moment of each blow, he found he could not move his feet.

Buckley sprang to her feet in time to see the smile dissipate from his face. With the same speed and force, she connected with the brachial plexus in his left arm, followed by his right.

Buckley took a step back and within a span of five seconds the attack was over. Vann found that he had lost feeling in both of his arms, similar to the feelings that overtook his legs.

He willed his arms to reach out and grab this woman, but they ignored his commands. His brain sent commands to his legs to kick the woman in her abdomen, but again, nothing happened. "You bitch!" he shouted, "What have you done to me?"

Buckley continued, "You see, Walter Vann, I do not serve men. Furthermore, I do not like to be interrupted." She walked with a deliberate purpose around him so that she could once again face the remainder of the group.

"I don't believe in wasting words; therefore, everything that is said should have some purpose. Mr. Vann, you have a nasty habit of running off at the mouth with no end goal in mind."

She looked out over the assembly, satisfied that all eyes were focused on each word coming out of her mouth.

I'm also precise in my action, so everything I do has a purpose. Did you know the body is comprised of several different pressure points? On the midline of the inner thigh, between the knee and the groin, sits your sciatic nerve."

Vann thought back to when the woman dropped to her knees. He imagined he was in for some pleasurable action similar to what the girls he trafficked did on a regular basis. However, he realized this was a method for her to gain the access she needed.

"My favorite is the brachial plexus. This particular pressure point has so many potential outcomes. Right now, you brain has quit communicating with your shoulders thus making your arms useless."

"Undo this right now, you damn whore."

"You're right, Mr. Vann. I should put you out of your misery."

She extracted the Tac Force spring-activated knife from her pocket, extended the blade and buried it in the base of his neck severing his spinal cord. His body went limp, and he fell face-first like a sack of potatoes.

Buckley wiped the blade on her jeans before retracting it in place. She tossed the switchblade underhand to Francene, who in turn caught it in shock.

She glanced at the knife that was used to kill Walter Vann, stunned to realize it was hers. *How did she get my knife?*

The crowd was silent as she made her way back to the stand. "If there are no further questions, we can now get started."

5

Veronica King sat at Nikki Smith's, a restaurant inside the country club, drinking her second glass of iced tea. Irritated, she looked down at her watch again fuming at the tardiness of Lydia. She made it clear to the woman that she wanted to meet her at 9 a.m., and with this last glance at her watch it was now 9:35.

She noticed motion moving in her direction, but it was only the waiter, William. He made several appearances to refill her drink and to inquire about her breakfast order. On each visit she kindly reminded him that she was waiting on a companion at which point she would order breakfast. It's obvious he didn't receive the hint that she wanted to be left alone because on cue he was approaching her again.

Treating the wait staff with respect was something Veronica believed in, but this morning she was on the edge. Lydia obviously blew her off, she would need to rectify this later, and the waiter's constant pestering was the final straw.

With each step he took in her direction, she calculated the words she would use to tear him down. She would probably feel bad about it later, but at this moment it's what she needed. She decided she would wait on him to inquire about her drink and breakfast once again, and then she would light into him.

Mentally she counted the paces, *eight, seven, six,* until he would arrive at her table. With five steps remaining, he would go into his cheery, "Can I offer you a refill? Would you like to hear today's specials?" routine.

He approached the table with his familiar smile, ready to launch into his questions.

She was armed and ready with her litany of premediated insults.

"Ms. King, this note was left for you," he said handing her a folded sheet of paper.

Veronica blinked her eyes a couple of times to wrap her head around this change of events. "A note," she said trying to regain her composure. *Who knew I was here?*

She took the suspicious note from William, curious of its contents. She unfolded the note and read the single line of text.

Ms. King, my black town car is awaiting your arrival outside. Lydia.

VERONICA WAS SHOCKED at the note and thought, *what the hell. She is now summoning me?!* For a minute she considered blowing off the request, but this wouldn't get her any closer to the answers she sought.

Reluctantly, she began to gather her belongings. From the corner of her eye, she could see William beginning to approach her once again. She laid a $20 bill on the table and upon their passing told him to keep the change.

SEVEN MINUTES after receiving her summons, Veronica found herself outside in search of the black town car. Her search came to an end when the car she was searching for eased to a stop next to her. She heard an audible click of the door lock disengaging. *Guess that means I'm supposed to get in*, she thought inhaling deeply before grasping the handle.

She opened the door to peek inside. "Have a seat, Ms. King," came the voice of Lydia Brooks who sat in the seat furthest from the door.

Veronica slid in, closing the door behind her. The locks clicked into place as the driver pulled away from the curb.

"Veronica," Lydia said turning to face her guest. "I was surprised to receive such a, shall we say, direct call from you this morning."

The confidence she felt when placing the call was replaced with apprehension, *have I gone too far?* She realized in that moment, no one knew where she was. She climbed into this car, not even aware of the destination. If she disappeared, her last known location would be the country club, primarily because her car would be found there.

Lydia's voice brought her back to the present, "What can I do for you today?" Veronica realized there was no turning back. She calmed herself before speaking. "I have done everything that has been asked of me, the majority of it I did under duress. Nonetheless, I did all of it. To make matters worse, I have been informed that I must work for a company, The Syndicate, that I know next to nothing about."

The expression on Lydia's face remained impassive. Veronica began to feel uncomfortable with each word she spoke, but she continued.

"I don't make a habit of working for people, or companies, that I don't know." She paused waiting to see if the woman sitting next to her would say anything.

When her companion offered no words, she pressed forward.

"Lydia," she said turning in her seat. "There is no turning back for me. I have made the decision to be a part of this, whatever this is. All I'm asking is for information on what I have gotten myself into."

"What exactly is it that you would like to know?"

"Who is The Syndicate? What is Syndicate? Who is in charge? When can I meet the person in charge? How can I take on a larger role within the organization?"

"Well," Lydia said turning in her own seat so she could face Veronica. "You do have a ton of questions. What do you plan to do with the knowledge you would gain from the answers to these questions?"

Veronica was prepared for this question, and now it was time for her sales pitch. "I excel in everything I touch. The more I know about the organization, and the leaders within the organization, the more value I can add. While some people strive to be an unknown worker bee at their company, I want to be the one driving the organization into the future."

During the entire sales pitch, Lydia's expression didn't change once. Veronica wondered if she had overstepped. If she played her cards too soon.

Lydia turned in her seat to face forward once again. Veronica watched as she pushed a button on the side of her door. The partition between the two of them and the driver turned a dark, smoke brown making it impossible for Veronica to see anything in front of her. Next, the passenger windows took on the same hue followed by the rear glass.

Veronica surveyed her surroundings realizing she could not see anything outside of her immediate setting.

Lydia depressed another button on the door. "Yes, Ms. Brooks?" came a voice over the speaker.

"Charles, please be a dear and drive us to the office. Normal precautions."

The office?! Normal precautions?! Where the hell is she taking me?

"Yes ma'am, Ms. Brooks."

The tiny, ambient sound from the speaker dissipated plunging the rear of the car into silence.

Lydia turned her head to address Veronica, "Please buckle your seatbelt."

6

Donatella walked into Brent's Coffee Shop on Trade Street taking in the aroma of fresh baked goods. This had become her home away from home when she needed a place to think free from interruptions.

The implications from the meeting with Brewer began to sink in once she left the office. He had been her silent ally in the hunt for The Syndicate. He gave her the latitude to pursue any lead no matter where it led. With a change in leadership there was no guarantee she would have the freedom that she enjoyed to this day.

"Chai tea latte," she said when she reached the counter to place her order. To her surprise, Margaret, the pink-haired girl who had become synonymous with her visits to Brent's, was not there today. *I guess everyone deserves a day off*, she mused.

She stepped to the side, allowing the next guest to be served while awaiting her order. In doing so, she ended up near the espresso machine. Steam began rising as the barista prepared another drink. Donatella could feel the tightening in her chest, heart pounding against her ribcage. She closed her eyes, willing her mind to realize that this was an irrational fear. When she opened them, the steam had vanished, and her vitals began to regulate. *I must get a handle on this.*

A second barista called out, "Donatella," and handed her the chai tea that she ordered along with a straw. She thanked him with a nod of the head before heading out to find a seat. As luck would have it, the shop was not crowded, and the oversized chair she preferred was available.

Donatella settled into the chair, placing her drink on the round table next to her. The stillness within the coffee shop enveloped her allowing her mind to drift into a meditative state. She thought back to another episode from her childhood.

DONATELLA AWOKE from the nightmare that played out in real life. Three weeks had passed since the death of her parents, two weeks since the funeral without their bodies.

Each night her nightmare brought her back to consciousness, sweating profusely, bed soaking wet, and tonight was no different. However, there was a foreign sound originating from down the hall.

Sleepily, she climbed from the bed rubbing her eyes to clear her vision. A sliver of light crept through the partially closed bedroom door.

The door groaned on old hinges as she pulled it open. Upon stepping into the hallway, she realized the illumination came from her aunt's room.

Since the death of her parents, her Aunt Susan had become her legal guardian.

Donatella moved in with her a few days after they received the news. To this point, her aunt had been the strong one. She took care of all the arrangements and she made sure Donatella had everything she needed. She even went so far as ensuring Donatella's room within her house had everything her own room had in her parents' house.

As Donatella moved closer to her aunt's room, she heard the sound again.

Adrenaline kicked in forcing her into action. She ran down the hall as fast as her 11-year- old body would take her and burst into the room. Eyes wide with fear she looked around realizing there was no intruder.

Her aunt looked back at her, eyes red, nose puffy, holding several tissues in her hand. Donatella realized this was the first time she'd witnessed her aunt cry other than the day she gave her the news.

Sheepishly, Donatella asked, "Aunty, are you ok?"

Wordlessly, her aunt shook her head in affirmation. She waved Donatella over with her right hand while calming herself to speak.

Donatella's feet felt like lead grounding her in place, but she succeeded in moving forward. She found herself in a tight embrace from her aunt as she continued to sob silently.

After a minute, Susan spoke, "I'm sorry, sweetheart. I'm so sorry this had to happen to you. I miss my sister, your mother, so much that sometimes grief overcomes me."

She dabbed her eyes once again with the tissue.

"We will get through this. We have to get through this. I will be there with you every step of the way."

Donatella pulled away from her aunt so that she could

look her square in the eyes. "Do you think they will catch the bad men that did this to my parents?"

"I know the police are doing everything possible to find those responsible. We have to trust they will and pray for justice."

Donatella contemplated this statement for a moment. With fire behind her hazelnut brown eyes she said, "If they can't find them, I will. And when I do find them, they'll wish they hadn't killed my parents."

Susan felt a cold shiver overcome her body. The look on Donatella's face was that of determination and she knew her niece would follow through on her declaration.

DONATELLA OPENED her eyes sensing a presence entering her space. When she did, Margaret was bent at the waist scrutinizing her.

"I'm so sorry, Special Agent Dabria. I didn't mean to wake you. You were so lifeless that I thought something bad had happened to you."

The look of concern receded from her facial features and was replaced by her familiar ear-to-ear smile.

Donatella smiled back at the charming woman. "My apologies," she said in her southern drawl. "I didn't mean to cause you any alarm. I was simply in a meditative state."

"Wow! I wish I could do that. If I close my eyes for more than five consecutive minutes, I fall fast asleep. Hopefully your meditation brought you some peace and relaxation."

"Thank you," Donatella responded. While meditation normally did these things to her, today's session only brought back some long-repressed feelings.

FRANCENE STOOD at the pump filling the car with diesel fuel. As the gallons ticked away she pondered the woman sitting at the wheel.

She told the assembled group at the warehouse to call her Terri. Over the next several weeks they would embark on a number of high-profile, well-coordinated attacks. She refused to provide any details to the attacks on the docket, only saying when it came time to execute the plan, they would be given more information.

Francene watched as the woman commanded the room, and to be more to the point, she commanded respect. After the quick, efficient way she dispensed of Walter Vann, there were quiet mummers within the group.

One of the men, Robert Nolan, tried to convince the group she had a hand in the kidnappings that took place within the Driftwood Springs neighborhood. Since he could not furnish any proof to substantiate his claim, it was dismissed as folklore and not brought up again.

Another group member, Juan Levine, believed from the way she handled herself when dealing with Walter, that she spent some time in the CIA. Again, no proof could be furnished therefore, he too, was dismissed.

The one irrefutable fact the assembled group could agree on was that she was not someone to take lightly, and she was not to be double-crossed. The speed, skill and fluid precision behind her movements was something they were not accustomed to in their perspective worlds. She was clearly cut from a different cloth, therefore their approach in dealing with her would need to be different.

The handle on the pump clicked denoting the tank was full. Francene positioned the nozzle back where it belonged while taking one last look into the convenient store. She wanted to go inside to grab a drink but Terri nixed the idea saying she didn't want her to be caught on camera.

Sure, there were cameras in the parking lot, but Terri assured her they would not be recording anything that took place outside at the pumps. She wanted to inquire why the outside was not recording but after seeing what she could do with their bank accounts, she figured she already knew the answer.

Giving up on the soda she desired, Francene climbed into the passenger seat. "We're all set to go," she said, buckling her seatbelt.

She decided to press her luck asking a question that she figured wouldn't be answered. "By the way, where are we headed? Seems we've been driving for a while."

Terri pulled away from the gas station, ignoring the question. Francene realized the woman had not spoken more than 10 words since they began this excursion.

She continued, "I guess I'll find out when we arrive. Do you mind if I turn the radio on?" she asked, searching for the power button.

Before she could make contact, Terri shot her hand out grasping the woman by the wrist. "Don't touch that."

The pressure Terri exerted within her grip left no room for discussion. Francene yanked her hand from her grip, "Geez, lighten up. You're not saying anything. I don't know where we are going, and I sure as hell don't plan on asking, 'are we there yet?' I guess I'll just sit here awaiting further instructions."

In a deadpan voice Terri said, "That would be a wise idea."

The next 20 minutes passed quietly without incident. The silence was broken when Terri pulled the car over to the curb stating, "We're here."

Francene looked around more confused than when they left at the onset of this trip.

They were in a residential neighborhood in suburbia. "Where exactly is here?"

To her surprise, Terri answered this question. "Before we can embark on the quest I have designed for the team, I need to address some unfinished personal business."

In her lifetime, Francene encountered two situations that caused her to shiver involuntarily. The expression on Terri's face, along with the hate behind her eyes, just marked the third such occasion.

"When we enter the property, your job is to detain, restrain, or eliminate any threat that is not the main target."

"The main target," she said in confusion. "Who is the main target?"

Opening the door and preparing to stand, she answered, "There will be no doubt, it's the person that I'll go after."

What kind of bullshit answer is that, she thought. *Could she be any more cryptic?* She opened her own car door and followed in Terri's wake.

Terri strode with a fierce determination in each step that she took. It could have been from the sun, but Francene swore there was a glow encasing Terri's body.

Within stride, and in one fluid motion, Terri kicked the door connecting with the handle. The door jamb splintered into several pieces as the door swung open on its hinges.

Terri moved toward the staircase and took the steps two at a time until she was at the top. Francene did her best to keep up while looking for any threats. None presented themselves so she kept moving.

Their trajectory had them on a path for the master suite. As they approached, a male voice emanated from behind the closed door. "I have a gun. Stay back." Undeterred, Terri continued on her path kicking through the closed door which gave way instantly.

Aaron Smithville stood on the other side, gun raised, finger on the trigger. "It's you," he said recognizing the figure who barged into his house and his bedroom.

SMITHVILLE SEXUALLY ASSAULTED Terri when she was a freshman in college. Although she did everything she could to block out the horrors of that encounter, she couldn't.

Several years ago, when she was an agent with the FBI, Terri discovered the whereabouts of Aaron. She broke into his residence prepared to shoot him for the heinous act he perpetrated against her. Her main agenda was to exact justice for her and all of the other women who are assaulted and never receive the justice they deserve.

However, her partner, Donatella, prevented her from pulling the trigger and thus enacting her revenge. This singular act was the catalyst of her feuded hatred with the "do nothing wrong, goody two shoes" agent.

He was arrested that night and charges were brought before the court. His defense attorney painted him as a loving, single parent to a beautiful little girl. A standup member within the community. A God-fearing, church-going man. He argued there was no evidence to support the victim's claim and reminded the court that the victim never sought the assistance of the law prior to breaking into his client's house to murder him.

Instead, she used her status within the FBI to track down his client, hold him and his daughter at gunpoint, and had it not been for the quick actions of her partner, both Aaron and his daughter may have been killed that evening.

Smithville was found not guilty of the charges brought before the court and he was a free man. Once again justice had been taken away from Terri and she swore he would pay one way or another for his crimes.

Smithville could hardly believe that the woman who tried to kill him several years ago was standing in front of him yet again. She had that same murderous intent in her eyes that she displayed the last time he saw her. The last time he found himself staring down the barrel of her gun.

But this time the tables were turned. He was the one who held the gun in his hands, and he already had the weapon pointed in her direction. He bought the gun for protection several years ago, but never figured he would be using it on the woman he had a good time with back in college.

"You, again," he said, giving her the once over. "What are you doing in my house?"

In a cold, undetached voice, she responded, "To deliver the justice you should have received during our last encounter."

He couldn't help but chuckle inwardly, and smirk outwardly. "Seems like the situation is a little different today. As I recall, last time you held the gun, and I was at your mercy."

He casually waved the gun back and forth. "This time I'm the one holding the gun, thus I'm the one holding all the cards."

He looked over her shoulder realizing Francene for the first time. "Once again I see you brought along a friend. What happened to the hot, curly-haired woman you came with last time? She was a feisty one. If it wasn't for her, I wouldn't be here today. I sure would like to thank her."

Her rage at its crescendo, she said, "Your time is up, Aaron." She sprinted across the room in his direction.

Shocked at her sudden movement, he pulled the trigger and nothing happened.

Terri swept the gun away with her left hand while punching Smithville in the throat with the clinched fist of her right hand. He crumbled to the ground like a puppet whose string had been cut.

She looked dispassionately at the man lying on the ground searching for his breath. "If you're going to threaten someone with a gun, make sure you know how to use it." She thumbed off the safety and fired it twice, one shot for each knee.

He screamed out in pain as the bullets tore through his flesh. As he did, Terri took the opportunity to execute the reason for her intrusion. With his mouth wide open, she pulled a plastic sphere from her pocket and forced it down his throat.

Involuntarily, he swallowed the foreign object. "You bitch! What have you done to me?" he grunted through gritted teeth.

She didn't answer. Instead, she turned her back and

calmly exited the room. "Let's go," she said to Francene, who hadn't taken a breath since the ordeal began.

Smithville released a torrent of expletives as the pair walked down the stairs and back out of the house. By the time they made it to the car, Aaron's words were replaced with abject screams of agony. Even with the door closed and the rumble of the engine, his screams could still be heard as they drove away.

Unable to resist any longer, Francene asked, "What on earth did you give to him?"

Terri's pupils returned to their normal state and her calm, calculated demeanor was present once again. Without turning to address her companion she responded, "Exactly what he deserved."

7

Inside the home of Marcellous and Jasmyn Thompson the smell of lemon-roasted chicken, sheet pan sautéed vegetables, and fresh baked bread wafted through the house. Ever since the couple brought home their first child, Sebastian, from the hospital they didn't feel like entertaining.

Donatella dropped by a couple times, the last being when she received the cryptic call from Terri Buckley. Other than that, their social life came to a halt.

However, today was going to be different. Sal Grandson, a journalist they were acquainted with through the tragedy within Driftwood Springs, sent them an invitation for a dinner party. The couple thought they read the invite incorrectly when the location for the dinner party was their house.

Along with the invitation was a handwritten note featuring elegant penmanship. The note stated renovations were being done to their apartment, but they had some news they needed to share with those closest to them.

Jasmyn, who Marcellous always said could be a matchmaker, felt the two had wedding bells in their future.

"What makes you so sure?" Marcellous asked trying to dig into his wife's thought process.

"Really, Marcellous? You cannot be serious. It's so obvious. Renovations are being done to their apartment. The soon to be Mrs. Salvatore Grandson sends a handwritten note."

"Wait one second," Marcellous interrupted, "How do you know she is the one who wrote the note?"

"Honey," she said in her child-correcting tone. "Have you seen Sal? Did you pay attention to the curls on some of the letters? Does Sal give off the impression that he would curl his letters?"

"Curly letters! That's your proof?"

"Yeah, that. Not to mention he is a journalist. I've had a glimpse at the Mead notebook that he carries around. It looks like someone tried to write with their non- dominate hand while using their pinky and their thumb."

The chime from the doorbell resonated through the house.

"Saved by the bell," Marcellous said while walking toward the foyer to open the door. Jasmyn blew him a kiss and gave him a Cheshire cat grin. "You know I'm right."

Marcellous smiled, conceding the truth but not giving her the satisfaction. He loved their playful banter, something he wouldn't trade for anything in the world.

He opened the door to find Sal standing next to Jane with a bottle of wine in his hand.

"Sal, Jane, come on in. Let me take that from you," he said gesturing to the wine. "Mr. Thompson," Jane said kissing him on each cheek. "Thank you for inviting us into your gorgeous home."

"Thank you," he said leading the couple into the kitchen.

"Oh my God, look at you!" Jane squealed when seeing Jasmyn. "Girl, you look phenomenal. No one would figure you recently gave birth to your first child. What's your secret?"

The two embraced followed by Jasmyn saying, "Thank you. I feel so worn down all the time with the feedings every two hours in the middle of the night. Today is the first day I've dressed in real clothes with a dab of makeup."

Jane took her by the arm, "What it sounds like to me is momma needs a drink. Let's fix that right now."

"So, Sal," Marcellous chimed in as the women departed in search of wine glasses. "Care to shed any light on the purpose of this special visit?"

"Well," he responded sheepishly. "I think I better wait on the ladies before I say anything." He looked around the house and into the family room. "Speaking of ladies, where is our formidable FBI agent? With Jane changing outfits three times before we could leave, I figured we'd be the last ones to arrive."

"Donatella called ahead letting us know she would be late. I suspect she should be here any minute." Marcellous lowered his voice conspiratorially, "You sure you don't want to tell me the news now?"

"Marcellous, my friend. One thing you never do is anger Jane, or any woman for that matter. They can make you pay in ways you've never considered."

"OK, OK, OK," he said throwing his hands up in mock surrender. "I'll wait until the mysterious reason for our gathering is announced."

The chime from the doorbell cascaded through the house once again.

"I've got it," Marcellous announced already making his way to the door. Sal took his departure as a moment to go grab himself a glass of wine.

Marcellous returned 30 seconds later, "Look who I found."

Donatella walked in looking more stunning than Sal could remember. Jane sat her glass on the island and raced over to greet the FBI agent.

While the two women shared a hug, Sal raised his glass, "Hey there, Donatella. Good to see you again."

"Come in, let me grab you a glass of wine." Under normal circumstances, Donatella would decline the proffered drink; however, tonight she sensed there was a big announcement brewing so she decided on one glass.

Jane returned handing Donatella a glass of wine before making her way around the island where Sal stood. Jasmyn walked over to Marcellous handing him his glass.

Jane started, "I know you're all wondering why we asked you here this evening.

Well, let me start by acknowledging and thanking you once again, Donatella."

She turned to face the FBI agent, "Sal here knows how to get himself into precarious situations, as all of us journalists do at times. But in this particular situation, had it not been for you, Sal would not be here today."

THE PREVIOUS FALL while writing about the child abductions within the Driftwood Springs community, Sal found himself in mortal danger from the person who orchestrated the entire set of events. If Donatella hadn't been there, and if she didn't fight through countless adversaries, he would have been killed in an explosion.

DONATELLA RETURNED the smile and nodded her head in appreciation.

"It was then," Jane picked back up, "That's when I realized how important Sal had become to me. It was then that I realized that he is the love of my life." She turned to face Sal, the smile on her face growing wider.

"So," she said pulling her hand from her pocket. "We wanted to announce to our friends that we are engaged to get married." She held up her hand to show the assembled group the diamond adorning her finger.

A chorus of congratulations, smiles, and hugs carried around the room. Jasmyn elbowed Marcellous in the ribs with an *I told you so* jab.

"Why don't we toast to the happy couple," Marcellous said holding up his glass followed by everyone else. "To the happy couple. May your union bring you many years of health, happiness, and prosperity." They all touched glasses with a clink before taking a drink.

"When is the big day?" Jasmyn inquired finishing off her drink.

"Well, Sal and I talked it over and decided that we don't want a big wedding. In fact, you're looking at the extent of the people we plan to invite. We don't need a big ceremony to vow that we will love, honor, and cherish each other from here on out." She leaned over to give Sal a kiss on the cheek.

"We also decided that we don't want to wait forever; so we will be saying our 'I dos' at the courthouse in two weeks."

Sal picked the conversation, "We both would be honored if you could make it to the ceremony."

Agreements came without a moment of hesitation.

"Looks like your glass is dry," Jane said smiling at Jasmyn. "Let's get you another one." She grabbed her by the arm in search of a new bottle to open.

"Sal, you old dog. I knew that was the reason for this gathering. Congrats, again. By the way, I told Jasmyn the announcement would be your engagement. She didn't believe me."

Donatella felt the phone vibrate in her pocket. She retrieved it, surprised to see Brewer's name on the screen. "Special Agent Dabria," she answered in her honeyed voice.

"It's Brewer. I received notification that Aaron Smithville was murdered in his home earlier this evening. From all accounts it's a gruesome crime scene. I'm sending you the address."

Donatella knew the answer before she asked, nonetheless she proceeded. "Do you think it was –"

"From everything I've heard, this appears to be her handy work. Stop by the scene and see if there are any clues you can find to establish her next steps."

"Will do, sir."

"And Donatella, be careful!"

8

The absence of scenery passing by outside of the moving vehicle made it impossible to determine where they were going. Veronica knew this was by design, and she was willing to play along, if it meant moving her closer to her end goal.

Lydia sat silently in the seat next to hers looking through her phone. On several occasions she thought about asking where they were headed but she knew a straight answer would not be forthcoming.

The driver slowed to turn, something he had already done on several occasions.

However, this time it was different. This time the driver came to a complete stop and she heard what she thought was a window going down. She strained her ears to hear the exchange in front of her, but the conversation was muffled.

Once again, the car was in motion, and she could feel her pulse racing. The time was quickly approaching for her to make another pitch. This time, she hoped the pitch was for the person in charge.

Veronica noticed a subtle movement from Lydia. The next thing she knew the dark smoke treatment that covered the windows began to disappear. When it did, Veronica was pleased to see something other than her muted reflection staring back at her.

Once her eyes adjusted to her surroundings, she found they were descending in a circular manner in what appeared to be a parking garage. Their descent was complete 30 seconds later. The faceless driver pulled into a parking space that was simply labeled "Reserved". The door lock disengaged followed by Lydia's voice.

"Please exit the vehicle. Once you do, walk straight ahead. The elevator doors will open automatically, and you'll be taken to your destination."

Veronica hesitated, pondering her fate before exiting the vehicle as instructed. Nonetheless, she opened the door and slid from her seat. The air felt damp and while looking around she didn't see any visible signs familiar to her. As she stood outside, she realized that her companion was still seated in the car.

I guess I'm on my own, she thought as she walked straight ahead as instructed. The longer she walked she realized that her eyes could not discern any doors leading to an elevator.

The town car she exited only a few moments prior, reversed out of the parking spot, heading back in the direction from which they had come.

Fear and desperation began creeping into her mind once again. No one knew where she was, and now she had been dropped off somewhere underground with no viable way of escape.

Every fiber of her being screamed at her to run. To find a

way back to the surface and never look back. But her feet kept moving her forward even though an elevator was not present.

She reached the end of the line standing face-to-face with a flat, grey wall. *I'm going to die here*, she thought contemplating her next actions.

Run back to where we came off of the circular decline. It took us roughly 30 seconds to complete the descent so I can be back at the top in 10 minutes tops. But who had the driver spoken to when he rolled down the window? Would this person hold me against my will? One step at a time. First, I need to get moving.

She turned around ready to execute her plan when a hiss sounded from behind her. For a moment she considered not turning back because whatever it was, it was likely bad news. Then she chided herself, *I have already come this far, so what's a little further?*

She spun on her heel to face the wall. To her surprise, it began to part vertically from top to bottom. She had to smile inwardly as she never thought to look for a seem at the top of the wall, which she was sure was the point.

Once the door reached the ground, she stepped into the car, the door closing behind her. She searched the interior for a button to press only to find that a one didn't exist. *Why am I not surprised?*

When the door was completely closed, the elevator began to ascend at a constant yet rapid speed. In that moment, she was pleased she hadn't eaten anything at the club because her stomach began to churn with the elevators dizzying speed.

The car slowed to a stop presumably at the floor for which she was meant to exit.

The door silently opened revealing an office space Veronica had not imagined. It was surprisingly normal in its appearance. The floor she entered had a receptionist awaiting the arrival of visitors - normal. There were office spaces visible beyond where the receptionist was seated - normal. People milled around beyond the closed doors busying themselves with work – again, normal.

However, upon closer inspection it was not as normal as she had thought. The signage typically present within all office spaces was missing. The receptionist area, while nice, didn't have any furniture for waiting guest. The thing that struck her most odd was the lack of handles on the doors. While not necessarily strange in general, this omission stuck out in her mind.

Her feet moved her in the direction of the receptionist who already wore a wide smile across her face.

"Ms. Veronica King," she said standing from her seat. "I'll take you back to your meeting room. Please follow me."

Before Veronica could mount any sort of protest, the woman walked up to the door where it retracted to both the right and the left allowing her entrance into the inner sanctum. Veronica followed not knowing what else she could do.

Once beyond the receptionist lobby, if she could even call it that, she surveyed the working area that lay before her. The monitors attached to the wall displayed the stock market ticker along with other financial broadcasts. Although each cubical wall was low, each monitor was protected with a privacy screen. The path they took to the conference room kept them on the periphery of the work underway within this nameless company. They turned a corner where the receptionist came face-to-face with a door that slid open upon her approach.

"Please take a seat," she said pointing to the chair located in the center of the room." Again, Veronica did as she was asked. As she settled into her accommodations the receptionist walked away with the door closing behind her.

After two minutes of sitting in the chair, curiosity began to get the best of King.

She stood up from the chair and walked back to the door. She expected, or rather hoped, it would open, but she was not surprised when it didn't.

"Ms. King, please have a seat," a voice instructed from behind her. She nearly had a heart attack when she heard the voice. She turned around surprised to see a woman sitting in the chair opposite to the one she was sitting in. *Where in the hell did this woman come from,* she thought trying to keep her heart from pounding through her chest.

When her eyes were able to regain focus, she realized that the woman sitting in the chair fit the silhouette of the woman who paid her a virtual visit inside her home.

"I understand you have questions for which you are seeking answers," the woman continued as Veronica made her way back to the chair. "Let me see if I can fill some of the gaps."

Veronica had a plethora of questions running through her mind. How long had they been watching her? Why had they been watching her? The list went on.

Nonetheless, she composed herself and started with, "Who is The Syndicate?"

After a few moments of interminable silence, she responded, "You shouldn't think of us as a who, but instead as a what. We operate in the shadows, righting wrongs, and in some cases, preventing catastrophic events. Did you hear about the Amtrak train derailment on the Salt Lake City, Utah to Chicago, Illinois route?"

She pondered this question before responding, "No."

"That's because it never happened. We caught chatter of a plot to ambush the train and we put an end to it." What the woman didn't state was they had a client they were protecting scheduled to travel on that train. They stumbled across the plot and by virtue of protecting their client, they stopped the attack.

She continued, "We have clients that seek our services when conventional methods of getting what they desire cannot be used. We take pride in our customer service, though in a small number of cases a client or two has left – unsatisfied."

Veronica felt there was more the woman could say, but she was holding back. Nonetheless she pressed.

"Who are you? What is your name?"

The mystery woman shooed away the question, "Names are unimportant at this time. However, for the sake of argument, you can call me Ms. Blue."

"Let me cut to the chase," Veronica said sitting up in her chair. "I was pulled into this alliance of ours, reluctantly. But now that I'm here I want to excel. My dues have been paid once in my career, and to be frank, I don't fancy paying them again."

Ms. Blue's expression didn't change, but Veronica could tell she was pondering her comments.

"Ms. King, if you haven't realized it yet, being employed by our organization isn't a job you obtain by completing the traditional interviewing process. While you worked up the corporate ladder to hold your current position, there is no such process here."

"I'm willing to do whatever it takes," she heard herself say before she realized it.

Ms. Blue searched her expression for deception but found none. She stood from her chair and began walking to the back of the room away from the entrance. "Follow me," she said while opening a door hidden within the wall. "We have much to discuss."

9

The subtle shift in the wind swirled around the stale warm air. No birds were singing, no wildlife was moving.

Special Agent Donatella Dabria extracted herself from her matte-colored Audi R8 Spyder. Her previous car, the R8 coupe, was totaled as it flipped several times after being rammed by a dump truck. A truck doing the bidding of Terri Buckley to prevent her from giving chase in a hostage situation.

Now, she was headed to the home of Aaron Smithville. He had proven himself to be a slippery character by the way he wiggled free from assault charges. Donatella had no doubt that the claims Terri levied against him were accurate. She felt the case the police had against him was solid even though she knew it was a long shot. Since the victim in the case, Buckley, didn't show at the trial, his lawyer also argued that his client had the right to face his accuser. At the conclusion of the case, he was found not guilty of the charges, something she knew would set Terri off.

For two years, the Bureau kept loose security around him figuring Terri would go after him again. However, at the end of the second year resources were redeployed and Smithville became a distant memory. At least a distant memory for the Bureau. Arriving on the scene it was clear that Terri didn't see things that way.

The crime scene tape stretched across the front entrance with the door hanging from the hinges. She found herself amazed at the damage as she continued on her approach.

From behind her she heard, "Special Agent Dabria," from a familiar voice. Walking away from one of the Bureau's fleet vehicles was SSA John Brewer.

Donatella couldn't hide her shock while observing her supervisor traverse the street with haste to catch up with her.

"John, what are you doing here?" she heard herself ask. While he had the right to visit any crime scene, it was rare that he did. In fact, this was the first time he ever joined her at a crime scene.

"Early reports from the police department indicated that this is the worst crime scene they've seen since the massacre at GIS the previous year. I needed to see it for myself. I have to observe how far off the reservation Buckley has strayed. There is a piece of me that feels responsible for her actions – her discontent."

"Sir," Donatella interrupted, "You cannot blame yourself for her actions. By all accounts she harbored this notion of revenge against Smithville for years. The fact that I prevented her from enacting that revenge, and then turning my back on her as a partner has more to do with her state than anything you could have done."

Although he knew Donatella was correct, it didn't make

him feel any better to know that one of the agents that he cultivated had gone rogue.

"Let's go take a look at her latest offense," he said walking toward the building.

Agent Dabria followed in the wake of Brewer as they approached the bustling crime scene.

An officer who appeared to be fresh from the academy stood post at the entrance. His badge, affixed above his left shirt pocket, had the unmistakable new metal shine. His hair showing underneath his patrolman's cap was perfectly tapered. He still sported the nick he received from shaving that morning, but his eyes were alert.

He eyed Dabria and Brewer as they approached the building. When he realized they were headed in his direction to access the crime scene he spoke. "I'm sorry this is an active investigation. I'm going to need you to stay behind the tape."

Brewer pulled his badge from his pocket. "I'm Special Agent Brewer and this is Special Agent Dabria. We will need to examine the scene."

The officer glanced at the badge before turning his attention to his visitors. His eyes shifted multiple times between the pair as he contemplated how to proceed. When it appeared that he had worked out a decision, a figure materialized in the doorway.

"Brewer, is that you?" came a husky voice. "Martin, step aside and let Special Agent Brewer and his colleague through."

Relief settled over the young officer's expression since the decision was made for him. He lifted the tape waving the agents through and went back to scanning the street with the same efficiency as before.

The owner of the voice, a burly man, head clean shaven with a patch of hair affixed to his chin, stepped from the doorway to greet the agents.

He extended his hand, "It's been two, three years since I last saw you in the field. Looks like you picked an interesting one to drop in on today." The two men shook hands.

"And who do you have with you today?" he inquired, extending his hand to Donatella.

She took the proffered hand, "Special Agent Donatella Dabria," she responded in her honeyed voice.

"Detective Brent Johnson. It's a pleasure to meet you, Agent Dabria. Why don't we go in and tour the crime scene? I hope you haven't eaten anything recently."

As they entered the house and began to climb the stairs, Donatella couldn't help but thinking about the meal that was interrupted so she could be here this evening.

Interruptions were the norm in her line of work, yet she still enjoyed moments of normalcy when she could receive them.

At the top of the stairs the crime scene techs could be seen busily working in the room at the end of the hall. The rancid smell of burning flesh lingered in the hall originating from the room. Donatella, who was familiar with the despicable scenes Buckley left behind, was not prepared for what she witnessed when she entered the master suite of Aaron Smithville.

In the center of the room the victim lay on his back. The dried blood stains cascading from the knees made it clear that he had been shot in both of them. His entire torso appeared to be charred beyond recognition. His ribcage, along with the other bones in his upper body, were liquified and no longer present. His mouth was grotesquely open with an infinite, silent yell.

Upon approaching the body, it was clear that whatever burned through Aaron Smithville stopped as it reached the floor, exposing just a hint of the floorboards.

The more Donatella looked at the scene, the more she was confused and confounded by what her eyes were telling her.

Johnson broke her train of thought, "Looks like the perpetrator incapacitated the victim by shooting him in both knees. Then they set him on fire leaving him to burn to his death. We are trying to identify the accelerant that was used to cause this much damage."

"Are you sure he was set on fire?" asked Donatella. "If he was set on fire, I would expect to see more of his body burned, including the area around him. Furthermore," she said pointing next to the body, "there are still fragments of his shirt lying next to his body."

Both Agent Brewer and Detective Johnson turned their gazes to where she was pointing.

"If I had to guess, it appears our Mr. Smithville was burned from the inside out." The room sat in silence for a moment until it was broken by Detective Johnson, "Well, hell!" he said wiping his forehead. "What on earth could cause someone to burn from the inside out?"

The two agents passed each other a look that was lost on the detective. A look that said, *we need to discuss this elsewhere.*

"That's an excellent question," Brewer stated. "I'm happy to make the resources of the FBI available to you to determine the cause of this fire."

Johnson eyed the agent realizing he never asked the most

obvious question, "I just may take you up on that offer, but I have to ask, what is the Bureau's interest in this case?"

Brewer didn't believe in nor condone lying to another member of law enforcement; however, in this situation he didn't believe telling the detective the complete truth would be beneficial. If he put the CMPD on the trail of Terri Buckley, things could become disastrous. Terri was quick and efficient to lash out if she felt cornered. No, for this situation he had to rely on Donatella catching and stopping Buckley before she could do additional damage.

While there was a risk that Johnson could find that Smithville was tried for rape, and Buckley was the victim, it was highly unlikely. The trial was closed, and the proceedings were sealed, all done at the request of Brewer.

"I heard some chatter about how unusual and bizarre the scene was surrounding this murder. It's rare we have those cases come across the desk of the Bureau, so I wanted to take a look for myself."

He knew his rationale was weak for wanting to be at the scene, and from the look he received from Johnson, the detective felt the same way. Instead of calling him out on the obvious lie, Johnson simply said, "On second thought, I will take you up on the assistance from your lab."

"Consider it done. I will send them over immediately to provide any assistance you need."

The two shook hands once again with Johnson squeezing a tad harder and holding on a bit longer. They locked eyes for a moment before Johnson released his hand.

Wordlessly, the two agents made their way back through the hallway proceeding to the exit. Once outside Brewer said, "Donatella, this can get out of hand fast. I need you to find

Buckley and put an end to this before more bodies are found."

Donatella nodded her head in understanding. She agreed that Buckley needed to be found as soon as possible. But she feared this may only be the opening salvo.

10

T he full moon once again began to illuminate the night as the partial cloud cover began to dissipate. Francene realized that this was the third time in the last 10 minutes it had reemerged after tucking itself behind the cloud cover. The drive back from the unknown house went much like it did on the drive to the house – silent.

The screams and agony from the dying man could still be heard echoing in her ears. It was unlike anything she had experienced in her lifetime, but her companion continued to operate as if nothing happened.

Her daze was interrupted when she noticed they were driving through a sleepy neighborhood. Focusing in on her surroundings she realized that they were in the South Park area.

"Did you bring the gear as ordered?" Buckley asked piercing the silence. "Yes," she croaked activating her vocal cords.

Buckley depressed the phone button on the steering

wheel, "Call Number Four," she said. The speakers in the car activated once the phone on the other end connected.

"Yes," came the response from a woman once the phone was answered. "We're here. Remember to kill the video feed and the alarm."

"20 seconds," came the reply from Molly.

Molly worked as the technical backup for Terri as part of the Cleveland Museum of Art heist. While Terri was not accustomed to working with, nor trusting, anyone after being stabbed in the back by her former FBI partner, she had taken a liking to the tech.

She was smart, precise, and intuitive. She was able to anticipate what needed to be done given the situation. She executed her tasks on time, and with perfection, a trait Terri held in the highest regard.

MOLLY JENKINS GREW up in Boston, MA where she was revered as the most gifted individual in her class. She excelled in all elements of STEAM which garnered recognition around the state.

Her family, a lower middle-class family, consisted of her brother, two sisters, and their single mother. She was the third oldest out of the four in which she often struggled to find her place in the family.

Their family struggled to make ends meet every week, nonetheless their mother did her best to care for her children. At age 15, her oldest sister began working at the local grocery. This move helped to bring more money into the house, but also solidified the family obtaining three square meals a day.

Molly watched as her mother worked late hours, while her sister went to school and held down 30 hours a week to help provide for the family.

Molly knew her superior intelligence was the way she could give back to her family. She would go to the college of her choice where she would excel in computer science, land a tech job, and help to bring her family out of the check-to-check poverty that they lived in.

The college of her choice while in high school was MIT. For her chosen profession, there was no college or institution better for expanding her mind into the world of possibilities.

She attended a summer program during her junior year of high school, taking a few college level classes to prepare for her inevitable acceptance. Her mother, who looked much older than her 41 years, was excited at the prospects of her daughter attending such a prestigious school of higher learning.

In Molly's eyes, everything was set, and the only thing left was to complete her senior year.

However, something changed at the conclusion of her junior year when she prepared to enter her final year of high school.

The second week into her senior year Molly returned home to see a letter sitting in the center of the table as if it was on display. Her mother sat at the head of the table with a smile plastered to her face.

Curious, Molly dropped her backpack at the door, rushed over to the table, and picked up the envelope. It was an admissions letter from MIT. She glanced over at her mom whose expected eyes screamed, *open it already.*

Fumbling with the flap, she managed to pry the letter open. She opened the letter and began to read.

DEAR MS. MOLLY JENKINS, thank you for your interest in the Massachusetts Institute of Technology. Each year we receive thousands of applicants from across the nation seeking admission. We strive to admit the best and brightest from a diverse background.

After careful consideration of your application, we are sorry to inform you...

MOLLY DROPPED the paper because she didn't need to read any further. The joy on her mother's face was replaced with concern.

"What is it honey?" she asked.

"I didn't get in," Molly responded, storming out of the kitchen running into her room. She dropped face first into her pillow to muffle the scream and the tears. With all her accolades she couldn't wrap her head around not being accepted. She decided this wasn't time for a pity party, she needed answers.

She retrieved her Chromebook from the desk next to her bed that her mother worked overtime for two months to buy. At the time she was so overwhelmed she broke down in tears. She fired up the browser and began her search. She found an article five minutes into her search.

MIT had been petitioned by a 15-year-old boy to gain admission after scoring perfect marks on both standardized college entrance exams. He was being hailed as the next child protégé, and after months of debate, the school granted his application for admission.

She read between the lines of the letter and the article. This sudden change meant the university would need to reconsider their forthcoming applicants, thus shrinking their scholarship pool by one.

She pondered the realization of the 15-year-old boy that had been accepted. Although she could never prove it, she felt that Bryce Jacobs had taken the scholarship, and admission, that was meant for her.

Molly kept tabs on Mr. Jacobs. She was surprised by how fast he completed his curriculum at MIT, finishing in just two years. He was receiving his degree when she was entering her second year at the University of Massachusetts. Shortly thereafter his trail became harder to follow.

However, she saw his name pop up in a warrant issued by the FBI in connection with a potential lottery scam. She waited with great anticipation to see his name spread across the headlines with him under arrest.

But to her amazement, nothing happened. No arrest, no newspaper article, nothing. The warrant was sealed and he still walked the streets. She figured some sort of deal was hatched between him and the FBI, but she couldn't prove it.

In her own life, things began to fall apart. Her mother finally worked herself into an early grave, and Molly had not become the technology guru she felt she was meant to be.

She held down a steady job, one that paid the bills but her drive, and desire, disappeared when she had to settle on attending UMass.

Her siblings all went their separate ways, only coming back together for their mother's funeral. Once the services concluded, they all dispersed, never coming together again. It had been years since she last heard from them, but it didn't bother her as much as she thought it would.

Being alone wasn't the worst thing that could happen to her. She didn't have to worry about anyone but herself, thus she could not let anyone down like she had done to her mother.

One day after she completed her shift, she walked out of the office toward her car to find a woman leaning against the driver side door.

Apprehensive, she continued walking while speaking to the stranger, "Hey, that's my car. Do you mind?" The question came out a bit more forceful than she had intended.

The stranger, a woman in her 20s, turned to face Molly. "Ms. Jenkins," she said locking eyes with her, "I've been waiting a long time to meet you."

Concerned registered across her features as she began to reach in her purse for the pepper spray she kept handy. While it was mainly meant to fight off a man who tried to attack her, she had no qualms about using it against a woman.

"No need to reach for the spray in your bag. I come in peace," the stranger stated, raising both hands in supplication. "I'm here just to talk. Well, to talk and to offer you a job that allows you to utilize the God-given skill you possess but have kept dormant for many years. Not to mention, the job pays more than you could ever make at the menial job you have today."

Her hand hovered above the handle grip of the spray. *How did the woman know I had pepper spray in my purse?* She discounted this as a simple guess. More frightening was the woman mentioning she'd been waiting to meet her. *And what is it she said about dormant talents?*

"Who are you?" she managed to ask, not sure what else to do.

"A friend," came the response from the stranger as she moved away from the vehicle. "One who will help you in exchange for your help. Why don't we walk across the street to the coffee shop where we can talk? I can fill you in on what the job has to offer at which time you can make a more informed decision."

The stranger began walking in the direction of the coffee shop and before Molly realized it, her hand was out of her purse and she was following along.

MOLLY CAME BACK on the line 20 seconds later, "The security system is offline and the feed has been looped. You are good to proceed." In the background she could hear Terri Buckley providing the next set of directions to the woman she had with her.

Molly was part of the team debrief held after the events at the Cleveland Museum of Art. Terri mentioned that Donatella seemed to have assistance which was something she'd never done previously. When Terri mentioned that the agent had technical assistance to overcome the security mechanisms that were installed, Molly began to suspect she knew who had assisted her, Bryce Jacobs.

She knew of all the techs that the FBI had on payroll and she was confident none of them could bypass the security. The picture began to crystalize in her mind. Instead of arresting Jacobs for his crimes against the lottery commission, he was on a secret payroll within the Bureau.

Although she didn't have any proof, she felt with every fiber in her being that he was the one behind the plans being foiled.

Instead of telling the group of her suspicions, she decided she would aid Terri in her plot to take down the vaunted FBI agent, and take down Bryce Jacobs at the same time.

Inside the two-story Toll Brothers chateau, Donatella Dabria sat quietly looking at a picture of her parents. There was still so much she wanted to say to them but would forever be robbed of that opportunity. Over time, the constant pain in her stomach from the loss of her parents subsided, but she never forgot.

When she looked around the opulence of the house, she recalled her shock during the reading of the will.

"AUNT SUSAN, why must I go into this meeting with the lawyer? Whatever he has to say, I'm sure he can send in a letter to the house."

"Well sweetheart, the reading of your parents' will is a legal matter. It's not something that can simply be conveyed in a letter. I promise I will be there every step of the way."

Donatella chewed on the statement for a while trying to determine what she should do. She knew that her aunt was correct. The real reason she didn't want to attend the reading was because it was just one more reminder that her parents were truly gone and never coming back.

"Be strong dear," she said with a gentle hand on her shoulder. "The reading will only take a few minutes. Afterward, we can go get some ice cream. Does that sound like a plan?"

"Can I have chocolate sprinkles?"

"Absolutely, and some hot fudge if you would like." "Ok," she said brightening just a little.

Susan pulled the door open where they were then greeted by a heavyset man with a blonde comb over.

"Susan, Donatella. Come on in and have a seat," he said brimming ear-to-ear. "I hate that we have to meet under such dire circumstances. The only solace I can offer is to ensure that the Last Will and Testament from your parents," he said looking at Donatella, "and your sister," he said shifting to Susan, "are carried out per their instructions."

"Thank you, Bartholomew," Susan said taking a seat as Donatella sat next to her. "Can I offer either of you anything to drink? Water, soda, coffee?"

"No thank you. We would like to proceed with the reading as expediently as possible if you don't mind."

"Yes, yes. Of course." He pulled a single sheet of paper from the folder that lay open on his desk.

We, Amare and Isabella Dabria, being of sound, mind and body confirm that this is our Last Will and Testament. We leave to our daughter, Donatella Dabria, the value of our stocks and our liquid cash in a trust that will be maintained by her aunt, Susan Yates, until her 21st birthday. The trust can be used by Susan to care for Donatella until she becomes of age."

Bartholomew paused for a moment stilling himself for what was next to come. "That is the end of the will as outlined and signed by your parents. The value of the stocks at the markets last closing along with the liquid cash assets is $9.3 million." Donatella sat speechless not sure what to say or if she should say anything at all.

Susan, on the other hand, nodded at the lawyer before speaking.

"Thank you, Bart. This is indeed an extremely thoughtful, and unexpected gesture, from my late sister and brother-in-law."

"Why yes," he stammered. "There are some signatures we will need from you, Ms. Yates. I assume you would like to keep the stocks in the market. The dividends alone should care for young Ms. Dabria's needs." He pulled another sheet of paper from the folder and turned toward Susan to sign.

"I'm sure that will be the case. Thank you once again," she said signing the paper that lay in front of her.

"Come on, Donatella. It's time for us to dive headfirst into an ice cream sundae with sprinkles."

Donatella, who hadn't said anything during this exchange had a thought that continued to run through her mind. While her powers of observations were just beginning to surface, she had the distinct feeling that Bartholomew seemed nervous. At the mention of sprinkles, she decided to let it go as the pair rose from their seats and headed to the exit.

. . .

THE CELLPHONE SITTING on Donatella's lap began to vibrate. She looked down at the screen, pressed the talk button, and placed the phone next to her ear.

"Hello, Bryce. What can I do for you today?"

"BJ," he said in his normal response. He waited for her to amend her greeting; however, after the silence stretched on, he continued.

"A package should be arriving at your door right about... now." He could hear the chime of the doorbell ringing from the other end of the phone.

Donatella walked through the foyer on her way to the front door. At the entrance she saw the all-to-comforting sight of her blue ocean breeze orchids standing proud in a glass vase by the door.

She opened the door in time to see the delivery man hopping back into his vehicle. She picked up the box, heavier than she expected, while balancing the phone to her ear.

"What's in the box BJ?"

"In due time," he said with a smirk emanating through his voice. "Bring me up on video chat and cast me to your TV. I can walk you through the gadgets you now have at your disposal."

It took her a few minutes to ensure everything was set up correctly, nonetheless she managed. The image of Bryce Jacobs was in full display on her 65-inch Sony TV.

"Ok, BJ," she said in an exasperated tone. "What's in the box?"

"Good to see you too, Agent Dabria. You know, would it kill you to ask how I'm doing every once in a while?"

"Bryce, the box."

"Ok fine, open it up." Inside the box she found a black case with a 10-digit code.

He relayed the necessary digits to which she entered in turn. When the last digit was entered the lock disengaged and she opened the lid.

Inside, she found a solid black shirt, a custom-made SIG Sauer P226 pistol, a retractable baton, and a set of Shinobi throwing knives. The assortment, aside from the shirt, was similar to her normal loadout.

"I know what you are thinking, and yes, this is your normal gear. Well, your normal gear, in principle. I took the liberty of customizing these items so you are the only one who can use them."

She raised a quizzical eyebrow.

"Take the pistol for example. It's been calibrated to fire only if it recognizes your heart rhythm and pulse. Even in a situation when your heartrate is elevated, and your adrenaline is spiking. Anyone else who attempts to fire the weapon will continue to cycle as if the weapon was empty.

Similarly, the only way to eject the magazine is if it's your heart rhythm holding the gun. An additional nifty feature has been added as voice control. If you are within 20 feet of your pistol and you say the words, 'fire now' the gun will fire a single shot."

Donatella picked up the gun realizing the empty weight had increased by only a fraction. By all indications, the pistol in her hand was exactly like the one issued by the FBI.

BJ continued, "The baton, similar to the gun, is connected to your heart rhythms with one additional change. Instead of flicking your wrist to activate the baton, all you need to do is squeeze the handle twice and the baton will extend. Utilizing the same command, the baton will retract."

Donatella pulled the baton from the case. With her hand firmly on the grip, she squeezed the handle twice, and on cue the baton extended. She repeated the command and the baton retracted.

BJ smiled as he watched the devices perform as expected. It was impossible to know that it would work in the affirmative until Donatella had her hands on the weapons. They were able to validate in the negative as no person was able to fire the gun or extract the baton until this moment.

"The Shinobi knives are a bit more complex. We couldn't stop someone from picking up the knives and throwing them, although we tried. So instead, they have been modified to release two additional blades that will fly in 45-degree angles from the central blade. If you press the hilt of the blade forward a quarter of an inch, the additional blades will release after traveling five feet."

She pulled one of the throwing knives from the case following the directions provided by BJ. She felt the precise movement as described.

"I'll take your word for it with the blades," she said placing it back with the others. "No worries, we had plenty of time to test them out and they work as advertised."

"Now for the new piece of equipment, the shirt."

She picked up the shirt and said, "I'm guessing this isn't a normal shirt."

"You would be correct," he responded with a wider smile on his face.

The garment was deceptively heavy as compared to its appearance.

"Say hello to your new best friend. In your box you have seven machine-crafted Kevlar t-shirts. While the weight is certainly heavier than your garden-variety t-shirt, it's lighter and less bulky than your typical bullet proof vest. It's comprised of five ultra-thin layers, two of which consist of Kevlar gel. After several iterations, we are satisfied that this engineered product will keep you safe while minimizing the effects on your speed."

She had to admit the shirt was lighter than her normal vest, and with its size, she could wear with it undetected on a daily basis.

"I have to say BJ, you've done some nice work. But I have to ask, why?"

The smile he wore on his face turned serious. "Because that psychopath, Terri Buckley, is still out there. Sooner or later, she will set her sights on you again. I wanted to make sure you had the tools at your disposal to deal out the most destruction while protecting yourself."

"Thank you, BJ. This is unexpected but appreciated." She had not yet told him of the call from Buckley, but somehow, she felt that he already knew.

They said their goodbyes before Donatella headed upstairs to stow her latest gear.

12

SSA Brewer sat in his office reflecting on his career. Growing up, being an FBI agent was the furthest thing from his mind. He initially believed he would become a basketball player; however, he never gained the aptitude to master the sport.

With that career choice moved to the background, he decided to rely on his intellectual prowess. Becoming a doctor was next on his list, but he soon realized his sometimes-gruff manner didn't allow for great bedside manner.

By the time he reached the university, he was still undecided on a major. He evaluated what he was good at and tried to translate that into a career. He sought the assistance of his counselor, but she was too busy to be bothered with his trivial problem.

Leaving from the walk-in appointment with his advisor that never materialized, Brewer overheard a presenter speaking about the ability to combine science, math, and intuition to solve four-dimensional problems.

He snuck into the back of the classroom, situated himself

in the chair-desk combo, and listened with undeterred attention. By the end of the lecture a scrawny, baby-faced Brewer rushed to the front of the room seeking out the professor.

"Hi, my name is Johnathan Brewer. I'm not a student in your class but I would like to enroll. This lecture has me wanting to know more. How can I join?" All of his questions came out in a jumbled rush.

The professor smiled at Brewer, "Slow down, young lad. I'm thrilled to know the lecture had a positive influence on you. I'm currently full for the semester, and this is a junior level course. What's your major?"

"I'm currently still undecided. Where does this class fit within the curriculum?" "Well, there are a number of majors that requires this class as the prerequisite for the next set of classes. Criminology is one of them."

Brewer and the professor, who he later learned was Professor Anthony Watson, carried on the conversation for another five minutes at which time Brewer was sold on his next direction.

Immediately after the interaction with Professor Watson, Brewer went and declared his major.

Throughout the duration of his college career, Brewer took three different classes from Watson. The two kept in touch over the years, and Brewer thought of Watson as a mentor.

When he completed his training to become an agent, Watson was there for the swearing in ceremony.

Tough times hit four years later when Watson became severely ill with prostate cancer. Brewer stood by his mentor's side doing everything he could to keep his spirits high.

However, four months after the diagnosis on an early Saturday morning, Watson passed away in his sleep.

BREWER PUT away the obituary he was now staring at, not realizing he had even picked it up. Each year on the anniversary of his death, Brewer made the trip to pay his respects.

A knock on the door brought him fully back to the present. He looked up to see his boss, Josh Peters, standing at the entrance.

Walking into the office he spoke, "Brewer, I'd like you to meet Jessica Lawson. Jessica, this is SSA John Brewer, the head of our Charlotte field office."

Walking into the office on the heels of Peters was a 5-foot 7-inch brunette dressed in a perfectly creased two-piece pant suit. She wore a blue blouse under her jacket, with her hair stopping just above her shoulders. She had a faint scar in the center of her forehead that was concealed by her makeup application.

She smiled, reaching out her hand, "SSA Brewer. It's such a pleasure to meet you. I have heard nothing but good things about you and the manner in which you run this field office."

Brewer shook the proffered hand, "It's a pleasure to meet you as well, Mrs. Lawson."

"Please, call me Jessica. And for the record, it's Ms. Lawson."

"Jessica has been identified as your replacement to run the Charlotte office. I brought her by so the two of you could meet before the official announcement. I have a call with the President's Chief of Staff, so I'm going to leave you two. Jessica," he said looking in her direction, "I'll meet you at the realtor's office in three hours."

He gave Brewer a pat on the back before making his exit and leaving the two agents alone.

"So," Brewer managed while thinking what to do with this unannounced guest. "Why don't you tell me a little about yourself as we tour the office space?"

"Sounds good to me but first, is there somewhere in this building that brews a nice cup of coffee?"

"Of course," he said lighting up with a smile. "Right this way."

TERRI PACED the first-floor office of the commercial building she was using as a base of operations. The vindication she thought she would feel by ending the life of Aaron Smithville was short-lived.

The sounds of him screaming in agony as she drove away from his residence filled her with an unbelievable high; however, by the time she moved onto her next objective the feeling had dissipated.

As she strolled back and forth within the office space, she longed for that feeling, that rush to overcome her again. But no matter how much she yearned to have that feeling, the more it alluded her. Although she didn't feel the high any longer, the fact that he was gone would suffice.

She checked off her mental checklist that was now 33 percent complete.

She realized that the next conquest on her list would

require more in-depth planning along with several different actors playing their roles.

Buckley received confirmation that phase one of the plan was kicking into high gear today. It was imperative that each element was executed as outlined, because it fed into the final act in this play. She refused to get ahead of herself like she had done so many times in the past. In doing so, her ultimate goal had not been achieved, something she would not endure again.

In a couple of hours, she would meet with her ragtag group. A group that was vital to the remainder of her plan, even if they were considered disposable. With the number of operators she had lost in her two previous plots to rid the world of Donatella Dabria, The Syndicate scaled back on the number of resources she could use.

While Terri understood the stance they had taken, it was still a blow she hadn't expected. Nonetheless, it forced her to realize it's not about the number of resources, but instead the functions they perform. Thus, she reconfigured her plan to maximize the resources she would have.

She smiled when she thought about the simplicity. She would not fail a third time!

THE SOUNDS of a little girl having a tea party with her stuffed animals bounced around the playroom. Veronica King stood silently watching as her daughter gave tea to her favorite stuffed animal, Victor, a big black bear.

She couldn't help but notice how well-adjusted she had become with the absence of her father. To Veronica's delight, she seemed to have forgotten about the cheating bastard who was rotting at some undisclosed location.

In her mind everything was still surreal. A stranger, who she now knows as Terri Buckley, forced her way into Veronica's office with an ultimatum. The Syndicate would knock off her husband who was in the process of leaving the country with her daughter and his mistress. In exchange, she would have to murder the board of her company who had a meeting scheduled for that day. The hitch, if she refused, they would let the plane take off, and then set off an explosion while the plane was in flight killing all passengers on board, including her daughter.

In reality, there was no choice. She was not going to let her daughter die in a premeditated attack when she had the opportunity to save her. To Veronica King, every decision she made from that moment on was aimed at saving her daughter. Well, almost every decision.

Her meeting with Ms. Blue left her head spinning. While she was not firmly cemented within the inner sanctum, she wasn't completely on the outside any longer.

She also looked at Terri Buckley differently now. Prior to the meeting, she felt this woman wielded all of the power; however, learning more about their structure helped her to realize that Terri wasn't as important as she thought.

Sure, she was efficient in performing her duties, but she didn't make final decisions. Plus, her obsession with the FBI woman seemed to be causing friction with the higher ups. It was made clear that their frustrations with her were something they would not tolerate much longer. Veronica wasn't 100 percent sure what this meant, but it didn't seem like The

Syndicate had a retirement plan for resources in that position.

While she had become fond of Terri, she would not allow their connection to stunt her upward growth. She made the tough call with her husband, Kyle, a few months prior, and she had no reservations on making a tough call again, should it come to that.

"So, LET ME GET THIS STRAIGHT," Jessica said sitting in the chair across from Brewer. "The suspect was hiding in his tool-shed completely naked?" she asked and burst into laughter once again.

"Yes, he was. Once he was cuffed and posed no additional threat to the community, we asked his wife to bring him some clothes from inside the house. To this day it's one of the most bizarre cases I have worked as an agent."

"I'd say. I'm not sure what I would have done. You never know what you will be faced with when doing this job." She sat her coffee cup on his desk fixating on him with her brown eyes.

"Let's broach a subject we haven't touched on yet. You had an agent," she looked down at her notes, "Terri Buckley, who turned out to be a bad seed. Given everything I have heard about her, I'm surprised she passed the psych eval and made it into the Bureau. Nonetheless, I'd like to hear from you about her and this apparent feud she has with," she consulted her notes once again, "Special Agent Dabria."

Brewer knew it was a matter of time until this topic was brought up. Throughout their tour of the building, he pondered the best way to address the dynamic between the two and their sorted history.

How does one put into words the story of an agent who tried to murder a civilian? A murder she planned to carry out in front of his child; nonetheless, only to succeed recently. How do you convey that Buckley's initial attempt was thwarted by her partner which leads into to unprecedented hatred? How do you explain this former agent has joined forces with a shadow organization responsible for the death of her former partner's parents? An organization that provides her resources to carry out her vendetta as long as she does their bidding as well.

How do you explain that you have allowed the other agent in question, Donatella, to track her parents' killers? A decision you made because you, too, have been affected by this same shadow organization. How do you justify allowing this agent to be the only agent in the office to investigate cases without a partner? It goes a lot easier when the agent in question has the highest closure rate in the office and within the Bureau.

Brewer sat back in his chair, arms above his head as he formed an answer to her question. "Well, that is an easy question with a complicated answer. I think we are going to need more coffee before we dig into their history."

"Well, I guess you better lead the way," Jessica said, standing from her seat. "Sounds like we have a lot to discuss."

13

A s the dusk settled across the city, Sal sat in the counter-height chair at his newly minted dinette. This day, like many others over the past few weeks, was filled more with wedding prep than journalistic writing.

He lamented of how much simpler his life had been before he decided to pop the question to Jane. He had the house to himself. He religiously worked out every morning, something he found that he could now only manage to do three times a week. And the clincher in all of this, he had lost his favorite dinette with his favorite chair.

Sal felt everything in his life was slipping away. But he had to admit that there had been some improvements to his life as well.

Every night he slept next to a gorgeous woman who challenged him unlike any other woman had been able to do. His selection in culinary cuisine had drastically shifted away from takeout to more balanced meals. And although he wasn't working out as much, the changes in his diet had him dropping weight.

He shifted in his chair, the new chair, that he had to admit was more comfortable than the one he gave up. It was even easier to stand from compared to the lower set he was forced to get rid of. For all the complaining that he did, Sal had to be honest with himself, *she makes me a better man.*

Tonight, he was staring at the official invites they would be sending to their friends for the wedding. Although it was going to be a small affair performed at the courthouse, Jane wanted invites to be sent to those who would be attending.

The invites, a modern black and white design, cordially invited the guests to the union of Salvatore Grandson and Jane Markowitz. The reception would be held back at the apartment of the newly wedded couple.

He still cringed when he thought about having more than two additional bodies in his apartment, but nonetheless he rolled with it.

He stuffed the last invite into the envelope, sealed it with the self-adhesive, and sat it with the others.

"Well, Sal old boy, a week from Sunday you'll be fully hitched to Jane. Ain't no turning back." He made this comment out loud to himself, something he had been doing for ages. He knew it would be best to stop doing so as it had gotten him into trouble more times than he could count, but he found it was harder said than done.

In another moment of honest clarity, he knew he didn't want to turn back. In his heart he knew Jane was the woman for him from the first day they met.

THE CHARLOTTE SKYLINE twinkled an array of colors from the Uptown skyscrapers.

The city was abuzz as the evenings last pre-season game drummed along in the background. The Panthers were picked to win the NFC South this year behind a strong running game and a top five defense.

Donatella found traveling through Uptown more difficult than normal as she headed to the FBI building. Brewer requested that she stop in again. She figured he had an update on his replacement and wanted to tell her face to face. More than that, she was sure he wanted an update on the hunt for Terri.

To her surprise, the former agent had been suspiciously quiet. This worried Donatella on several levels because she knew this meant the former agent was likely planning her next move. A move that would surely mean a method of destruction that only Terri could dream up. Donatella knew she needed to get ahead of her former partner's new plan, but she wasn't sure where to begin.

When the elevator stopped on the fifth floor, Donatella saw Brewer sitting in one of the cubicles staring into space. This was the most relaxed she'd seen her boss in all the years they'd worked together. He stood on her approach pulling out a chair for her to sit in.

"A southern gentleman," she said nodding her head forward in appreciation prior to taking a seat.

He smiled in response. "Thank you for stopping by this evening. I hope I didn't pull you away from another engagement." Brewer didn't make a habit of delving too much into his agents' personal lives unless they were willing to share unprovoked. Nonetheless, he knew Donatella had been preoccupied with her recovery in addition to looking for members of The Syndicate.

She shooed the comment away, "Nothing pressing. So, what do you have for me?"

Again, the smile creased his features, "Straight to the point as usual. I should expect nothing less. Anyway, it looks like the brass has chosen my replacement. A Special Agent Jessica Lawson. I had a chance to meet her today."

Donatella raised an eyebrow, "What did you think of her?"

"Smart, competent, charming, and tough. I think she has everything to be a good leader, and to carry this office to even greater heights."

Donatella was shocked by what she heard. Brewer didn't pass out compliments often, especially for those he recently met.

"She asked a lot of good questions during our time together. She also walked me through her vision for the office. Frankly, some of her suggestions were things I wish I would have thought of a long time ago. I truly believe her out-of-the-box thinking will be a benefit to the entire staff."

He cleared his throat, "We discussed you and Terri at length. I walked her through the history between you two. I stopped short of conversations concerning The Syndicate and Terri's new alliance with them."

Brewer shifted uncomfortably in his seat as he prepared for the next part of the conversation.

"We also spent some time talking about you. She didn't come right out and say it, but I think she plans to reel you in. She mentioned she didn't like freelancers under her command, and I got the distinct impression that comment was aimed squarely at you."

Donatella stayed silent. She wasn't surprised by the comment. In fact, she fully expected this would be the case. However, she had no intention of changing, something she felt Brewer could sense.

"Now, Donatella, you have to play nice. At least in the beginning. Give her a chance. You never know, you just may like her."

For Brewer, she would give Special Agent Lawson a chance, but she made no promises that she would like her.

"As you wish."

He knew that was the best he would get from her at this moment. "There are two more reasons I brought you here this evening," Brewer stated.

Donatella figured she knew where this was headed, none-theless she would hear him out.

"Special Agent Dabria," he said stilling his voice. "It's imperative we put this saga with Terri Buckley to an end. The killing of Aaron Smithville is likely just the beginning. Have you made any progress in finding her whereabouts?"

"Not at present. As you know, Buckley doesn't keep too many friends. The only people we know she regularly deals with is The Syndicate, and they are even harder to trace than she is."

Brewer shook his head knowing that she was right. But there had to be a connection, a thread they could pull, that would lead to her.

"What about the CEO of GIS?" he asked grasping at straws. "What about her?"

"In our debrief from your last case, you felt that the CEO

was being, shall I say, secretive. She is the only connection we may have to Buckley."

Donatella thought about it for a second. She recalled the ultimatum she made to Veronica King. The one in which she told her to decide if she wanted to seal her fate with that of The Syndicate. The one in which she nearly came unhinged at the manner in which this woman had so cavalierly killed her colleagues.

"It's a thread I can tug, but I'm not sure much will come from the discussion. She made it clear where she stood when the battle lines were drawn."

"That may be, but I still recommend pursuing her to see what knowledge she may have regarding Buckley's whereabouts."

Donatella nodded her head in agreement. "Is there anything else you need from me, sir?"

With the unpleasant conversations out of the way, Brewer smiled and said, "Yes, there is one more thing. The brass is adamant I will have a retirement celebration. I've done my best to persuade them it's not necessary, but they refuse to listen."

He slid a partially ripped envelope across the desk to Donatella. She picked it up, extracted the contents within, and silently read the elegant writing on the card. As she read, she couldn't help but feel amused.

"I know you want to laugh, but it's not funny. Against my wishes they have sent out invitations to the entire department. So now a week from Sunday, I will be paraded out in front of the entire office, and my wife, to be celebrated for the job I have done. You know I hate being the center of attention."

Handing him back the envelope she said, "That's exactly why they are doing it. You deserve to be recognized for how you have led this office. You should also be recognized for the career you have led. One of honor, integrity, and leadership. We could not have asked for a better leader."

The words of affirmation from one of his best agents meant the world to him. He was going to miss working with her. She was intellectually astute while being a force to reckon with in everything she did.

"Well, you can always go and accept the accolades and well wishes on my behalf." "Sorry, boss," she said standing up. "That's not how it works. You'll be fine, but just in case we'll have the paramedics on standby."

As she walked to the exit, he said to her departing form, "That may not be a bad idea."

14

Robert Nolan and his crew stood at the entrance of Bank of America stadium, home of the Carolina Panthers. He was assured by the woman pulling the strings of this operation that the credentials would work. He wasn't one for placing blind trust into someone he didn't know or trust. But if he was honest with himself, that woman scared the shit out of him.

He was a hardened criminal and did his share of dirt to ascend to where he was now, but this woman was different. The way she dispatched of Walter Vann was quick, efficient, and brutal. He was sure he didn't want to be on the other end of her wrath. If it wasn't for the money she'd promised for the job, he would have walked away.

When she presented him with the credentials, he asked how she obtained them. She blew off his question before reminding him of the time he needed to arrive at the stadium. He was also reminded of the trucks location that held the materials needed to complete the job. Above all else, she reminded him of the penalty for failure.

Prior to leaving to pick up the truck, Francene pulled him aside.

"I'D DO what she said to the letter if I were you." "Who the hell died and made you queen?"

"Relax, I'm just trying to give you some friendly advice. You remember what she did to Walter, well that was nothing compared to what she did on the trip she took me on."

She relayed the details of the encounter with Smithville ending with, "As we drove away, I could hear his cries through the closed windows. I don't know what she forced down his throat, but whatever it was, from the sounds of his agony, I think Vann got off easy."

Robert's faced turn pale from the play-by-play but he attempted to play it off. "She then took me to a house in the South Park area. I'm not sure who she was communicating with, but they defeated the security system within a matter of seconds. Once the system was defeated, we hopped the gate."

She leaned in, conspiratorially lowering her voice, "We ran around to the side of the home. I was scared to death that the motion sensors affixed to the home would go off. But for each one we passed, they stayed dormant. I could feel my heart pounding through my chest. For any heist I've done in the past, I had time to scout, and to determine my best course of action. In this one, I was flying by the seat of my pants relying on this woman, who less than an hour prior murdered a man without blinking an eye."

She wiped her perspiring hands on her jeans. "Once inside the house, she moved with elegance and stealth. She was decisive with fluid movements even in the complete darkness. When we arrived at what appeared to be a study, she immediately moved to the safe. 'You have five minutes.'

A dry lump was stuck in my throat. I could feel my hands shaking before pulling the tools from my bag. It was a good thing she had moved to keep an eye on the door because if she stood over me, I'm sure I would have failed at opening the safe. Nonetheless, with about 20 seconds left the door swung open."

Again, she wiped her hands on her jeans.

"She walked back over to the safe, pulled out a badge that was tucked near the back, and placed another call to the unknown person she had spoken to earlier. From the bag she was carrying she pulled a device that looked like a credit card reader. She inserted the card from the safe into the device. A few minutes later a green light appeared on the device. She removed the card, handed it back to me, and said, 'Close it up and let's go'. I placed the card back in the safe, closed the door, spun the wheel, and followed in her footsteps."

She sat back with her voice still lowered. "By the time we arrived back here an ominous black envelop sat on her desk. When she opened it, I saw a replica to the badge I observed at the house. It's the badge you now hold in your hands."

Francene stood up to walk out of the room. "Like I said, I would not fail if I were you. She has proven on several occasions she is not to be toyed with."

THE VISION of Francene walking out the door was still stuck in his mind. It was now or never. He placed the badge next to the reader. It stayed red longer than he felt was necessary, and panic began to set in. However, the light illuminated green and he heard the magnetic latch disengage.

He breathed a sigh of relief, *thank God*. He reviewed the floor map one more time before entering the building. With haste he proceeded down the long corridor, making a left at the bend. He flicked on the flashlight looking for the button that was to be affixed to the right side of the wall. What he expected to be a button extruding from the wall, was actually a flush button that nearly blended with the surrounding. Had it been a prison gray like the remainder of the concrete wall, he would have missed it. But it was red, and he was able to spot it on his second pass.

He walked up to the wall, pressed the button, and the satisfying sound of the chains rattling filled the air. When the doors were completely open, he waved the trucks through the opening, guiding them into place. After the driver jumped out of the truck cabin, Robert said, "Let's go, we don't have any time to waste."

15

The aroma of roasted brussels sprouts, yellow squash, fingerling potatoes, and chicken breasts drizzled with a homemade Asian sauce spread across the kitchen when the oven door opened. When short on time, a sheet pan meal was a fallback for Veronica. This was her third different variation, and thus far she was satisfied with each one.

Realizing the meal needed another ten minutes she closed the oven door while checking the clock. This gave her time to pour another glass of wine. It was her second glass of the evening, but after the day she had she felt having only two at this point was a win.

She filled her glass, which was almost empty, took a sip and savored the taste of aged grapes as their flavored danced on her taste buds. Her reverie came to an end with the ringing of the doorbell.

She sat the glass on the table, wondering if it was Terri. She had not seen her in a few days, which wasn't uncommon.

Nonetheless, she wondered what the woman had been doing to occupy her time.

Upon opening the door, she was shocked to see Special Agent Dabria standing at the door. She was typically cool under pressure and wouldn't panic; however, she was flummoxed at her appearance.

"Special Agent Dabria, to what do I owe the honor of you darkening the doorstep of my home, uninvited?"

The last time Veronica was face-to-face with Donatella, the agent was being escorted from the CEO's office by security. She made it clear that Veronica was to make a decision. A decision to admit what she knew concerning the executions at her office or to become a sworn enemy of hers. Veronica thought through her options and opted to keep her mouth shut.

As she looked over the features of the special agent, she couldn't help but to recall a resemblance, but she couldn't place her finger on who or why. The shape and intensity of the eyes are what drew her attention.

"Mind if I come in?" Donatella asked breaking Veronica's thought process. "You still didn't answer my question, why are you here?"

"We have some topics to cover concerning your involvement with Terri Buckley."

Hoping her face didn't betray her, she said, "I've already told you the last time we had this conversation, I –"

"What you told me, Veronica, was a lie. Let's stop kidding ourselves. We both know that the two of you crossed paths last year. I don't know why you are protecting her, or what hold she has over you, but she continues to play a dangerous game in which people are getting killed."

Veronica didn't know everything Terri was doing, and she was under no illusion that the woman was a saint. However, she knew if Terri was running a job, it was likely at the behest of The Syndicate, the outfit she was working hard to infiltrate.

"My guess is she is somewhere close. Considering she doesn't strike me as one to keep friends, she would likely turn to someone she has used in the past. That, Ms. King, would be you."

Veronica wasn't sure if she should be offended or flattered. "Agent Dabria, I'm not sure why you have this fantasy in your head, but I don't know her, I haven't seen her, and I don't know where she is. As an FBI agent I thought the Bureau specialized in finding people. Seems to me you are in the wrong line of work if you are asking for my help to find one woman who you claim has no connections."

Feeling satisfied with herself, she continued, "Now if you don't mind, I have dinner in the oven for myself and my daughter and I don't want it to burn. And next time, don't stop by my house unannounced unless it's with a warrant."

She closed the door with a smug look of satisfaction on her face. She was concerned that after all of this time the agent was still stalking around, but she felt she could continue to handle her.

Back at the kitchen, she pulled the sheet pan from the oven.

"Smells good," an uninvited voice pressed into her ear. "I love the way you dealt with Agent Dabria."

Veronica nearly dropped the pan but managed to maintain her grip. She turned to see Terri Buckley standing over by the coffee pot. Once again, the woman materialized within her home and she still didn't know how she was doing it. She placed the pan on the island as it seemed to have increased in weight.

"It's good to know I can still trust you. Because once trust is gone, what are we left with?"

"Well, I did it for my own self-interest more than yours. There are things I've done that I don't want her knowing about."

Buckley pulled a fingerling potato from the pan, "Like visiting the headquarters of The Syndicate. I'm not sure how she would have responded, but I'm sure it would not have been favorable."

She took a bite of the potato, "Needs salt."

How did she know I went to their headquarters? Did someone tell her I was there? Or worse, is she having me followed?

"I'll bring some to the table, assuming you're staying for dinner. It's been days since I saw you last. What have you been up to?"

She asked the question out of curiosity, and to also divert the conversation from herself.

Terri slipped off the lightweight black jacket and folded it in half lengthwise before tossing it on the back of the chair. She casually walked over to Veronica encroaching on her personal space. She could sense the other woman's breathing increase.

"Interested in my work now, are we?" She took another step now only inches from Veronica. They both stood around the same height, so they were looking at each other eye-to-eye.

"Let's just say," she leaned in and kissed her on the right

cheek. "The plan I've been working on," she leaned in to kiss her on the other cheek. "Is coming together quite nicely."

She leaned in and kissed her fully on the lips. Tugging at Veronica's bottom lip as she pulled away. She concluded, "And nothing or no one is going to stand in my way." Veronica saw a flicker of resolute determination and hatred in Terri's eyes. At that moment she wasn't sure if she was just threatened or not but she knew one thing for sure, she had better tread lightly.

"I'll set the table," she said catching her breath again. "Can I offer you something to drink?"

"I'll have some of that wine you are drinking. It's been one hell of a day."

16

R obert Nolan and his team finished unloading the materials they needed from the truck and onto the carts.

"This is where we go our separate ways. Marcus, I'm counting on you to lead the team. Follow the map along with the attached instructions to the letter. Trust me, we don't want to cross this employer. I've seen firsthand how she deals with failure. It's not a pretty sight."

"No worries, boss. I've got it. We will meet at the south entrance when we are done and then we can get the hell out of here. Are you sure you don't want one of us to go with you?"

"I'm sure. We don't have enough bodies to spare. It'll take all of you to complete the assignment if we stick to the timetable we have outlined."

Marcus felt uneasy about the arrangement but decided to go along with the program. He, along with the other four members of the crew, set off in search of their first destination while Nolan began his search.

Nolan held the forged keycard in his hand, "This had better work."

Terri, and the unseen voice on the other end of the phone, assured him everything was in order and they were specific in their instructions.

"WHEN YOU ENTER THE BUILDING, you'll need to find the main security room. The location of the room is marked on your map. The key we have given you will provide access into the room."

Terri chimed in, "You and your team need to be quick. While there typically isn't a guard walking the stadium, that doesn't mean that there won't be one there when you enter."

The unseen voiced picked up the thread, "When you enter the room, you'll need to look for the main server. It'll be the one with a keyboard and monitor attached to it. Insert the memory stick. It'll take a few minutes but the program installed on the stick will hack its way through the login sequence."

Nolan couldn't help but to feel as if this was some Charlie's Angels, Mission Impossible shit.

"Once you are beyond the login screen, locate the drive corresponding to the memory stick from the Windows menu. Open the drive and double click on the winking emoji."

A fucking winking emoji, he thought. *They have lost their minds*. The look he saw on Terri's face did nothing to assuage him of that thought.

·   ·   ·

AN INVOLUNTARY SHIVER shot through his body as he consulted the map.

"Right there," he said pointing across the hallway at the steel door. The door had a window that allowed him to look through. Empty.

Nolan pulled the badge from his pocket and placed it against the scanner. Unlike the door outside, this time the red light instantly turned green. He pulled on the door when he heard the magnetic lock disengage.

Inside he found a smaller control room that sat outside of the apparent server room. If he paid close enough attention, he would have noticed the cup of coffee sitting on the desk; however, he was so laser-focused on his task that the coffee melded into the background with everything else on the table.

He used the badge once again to enter the inner room. The temperature dropped some 20-30 degrees once he crossed the threshold, the door silently closed behind him.

Nolan walked the perimeter of the server room, but he didn't find the one with the keyboard and monitor as expected. Frustration began to mount when he noticed a gap at one of the racks that was bigger than the others. He walked over and examined the opening, immediately recognizing his mistake.

He tugged at the tray tucked under one of the pieces of hardware. He was rewarded with the keyboard and the flip up monitor that he had been searching for.

Nolan located the USB slot and attached the memory stick. Recalling the first portion of the lesson, he knew the device would now be overcoming the login screen. He looked around the room, *I could have worked in a cushy IT job. Seriously how hard could it be*, he thought.

He turned his attention back to the monitor when his peripheral vision detected a change on the screen. He was rewarded with the familiar desktop of a Windows machine. He had to give it to this Terri chick, she knew her stuff.

He opened a Windows Explorer window, found the attached drive, double clicked to open the contents, and found the winking emoji. In a macabre type of way, the emoji settled his nerves.

As the program began its work, Nolan was still clueless as to what it did. He was prepared to ask Terri, and the unseen voice on the other end of the phone, but he decided against it. Once he carried out this assignment, he would be paid. Knowing the details would only muddy the waters.

He figured it was some method to steal the money from concession sales, but that didn't account for the portion of the job that the rest of his team was carrying out. Again, best not to think about it. As the program did its thing, he heard the unmistakable sound of a magnetic lock disengaging.

"Shit! Who could that be?" He crept back over to the door and looked through the long, rectangular glass into the outer room.

Falling into the worn chair was an overweight, balding security guard wearing coke bottle glasses.

"Shit, shit, shit!" He walked back over to the monitor. The program was still running but the progress bar was stuck at 33 percent.

Stay cool, he told himself. *First things first. Let the program finish running. In the meantime, I need to figure out how to exit this room.*

In theory, Nolan would have enough time to devise a plan; however, Tiny, as he was known to his friends, had been working this security detail long enough to know when something wasn't right.

After sitting in his chair that groaned under his bulk, he noticed a glow emanating from the server room. Although the room wasn't completely dark, this glow was foreign, out of place.

He stood up from his seated position, walked over to the door, and took a look inside. Nothing seemed out of place from what he could see, but it certainly didn't feel right.

On the other side of the door, Nolan heard the approaching footsteps. He scurried around the corner praying the guard would stay outside. When he heard the inner door's magnetic lock disengage, he knew that would not be the case.

Tiny stepped into the server room, instantly feeling the drop in temperature. While others thought the room was too cold, he felt that the temperature was just right.

The server room had a set of racks directly in front of the door forcing you to turn left or right if you wanted to go further into the room. Tiny decided to go left.

He casually walked around looking for the source of the anomaly. In his mind, he turned into Detective Mike Lowery from the Bad Boys series when investing. He walked with a swagger while practicing his Lowery voice.

"Freeze, dirtbag!"

Hearing the voice, and the command, Robert Nolan froze in place. How had he been spotted? The guard was on the opposite side of the room. He then heard the same command in a different voice.

When he heard the voice and command for a third time, he realized the guard was practicing. He was able to track the guard by both his footsteps hammering out on the floor, and his constant command to "freeze".

He took another look at the progress bar, 62 percent. At this rate the guard would be over to the terminal before it was finished. As the guard grew closer Nolan needed to decide on a course of action. He was tucked away in the other isle, opposite from where he had been working. He had a 9mm tucked in the small of his back, but he didn't want to kill this man. He also knew if he didn't complete the job as directed, he was likely a dead man himself.

He looked at the screen once again and to his astonishment, the progress bar had jumped to 99 percent. He stared at the screen willing it to move to the final percent. He could hear the guard at the end, ready to turn the corner.

The progress bar concluded and was replaced with "Job Complete". He raced back across the aisle, snatched the memory stick from the USB slot, and darted through to the other end. He was turned around as he searched for the exit.

The guard was midway through his next "Freeze, dirtbag" when he stopped. *He must have noticed the keyboard and monitor.* After reorienting himself, Nolan picked up his pace to the exit.

"Someone must have left the monitor on earlier today. Although I don't recall seeing the light before my break."

Nolan could feel his heart pounding. Opening the door would make a sound and thus the attention of the guard. He silently prayed the guard would shut down the machine. They were still running an older version of Windows from what he could tell, and he hoped the shutdown chime was still present.

He waited with his hand on the handle ready to pull the door should he hear the familiar sound.

Sure enough, and right on cue, he heard the sound he was listening for. He yanked the door open, sprinted toward the door exiting the outer office and left as fast as he could, never looking back.

10 minutes later he was back at the loading dock where his team was assembled, "What took so long?"

"Nothing to worry about. Did you complete the installation as instructed?" "Sure did, boss."

"Good, let's get out of here. I'm ready to collect on this payday and never see our benefactor ever again."

17

D onatella Dabria stood in her foyer fixated on the blue ocean breeze orchids that were lovingly arranged in a customized vase. The orchids were a connection, the only connection, she still had to her mother – her parents. The fastidious care they needed to bloom successfully was something she didn't mind doing as it was a task her mother took on. A task that she later shared with Donatella prior to her death.

She could still recall the first time she planted them while living with her aunt.

"DONATELLA, sweetheart. What are you doing out here?"

"Aunt Susan," she responded, face full of innocence, eyes full of determination. "It's time I plant the ocean breeze orchids."

"Ah, yes. Those flowers caused me all kinds of grief growing up. Your mother worked at it until she perfected her technique. It took her a couple of years, but she finally mastered the technique and grew them on a regular basis."

"She taught me how to grow them before..." Donatella sheepishly said, as her voice trailed off and her eyes fell to the ground. She could sense the tears building behind them and she didn't want her aunt to see her crying again.

Sensing the dismay of her niece, Susan chimed in. "Oh, she did? No matter how much I tried, and how long she tried to teach me, I just couldn't get it right. But I'm willing to learn again from a new teacher if you'll have me as a student."

Although still young in age, Donatella knew what her aunt was doing, and she appreciated her for that. Lifting her eyes to meet her aunt's, she said, "I'm willing to give it a go, but I must warn you I won't allow any slacking."

A smile crept over her face as Susan feigned a scolded expression. "What do we do first, professor?"

DONATELLA SMILED AT THE MEMORY. For two years she worked at training her aunt how to care for the flowers, but Susan just didn't have the green thumb. However, in working to teach her aunt, she perfected her own technique. In doing so, she grew ever closer to her mom.

She turned to the helix-style staircase making her way up the left side. "Alexa, turn off ground floor." Simultaneously, the lights on the first floor turned off plunging the lower level into darkness.

Upstairs, she entered into the master suite as her mind transitioned to the endless battle with Terri Buckley. She was sure that Veronica King was lying but she had no basis to request a warrant.

Knowing that Buckley was out there planning her next move was maddening. She retrieved her cell phone from her pocket, found the number she was searching for, and placed the call. After two rings the phone was answered.

"Special Agent Dabria," the voice on the other end stammered out. "I didn't expect... um... what can I do for you?"

"We need to meet," she responded in a curt voice. "Tomorrow morning. 8 a.m." "Um. I can't tomorrow. I have –"

"Tomorrow morning, 8 a.m. Don't be late." She disconnected the call before placing the phone back into her pocket. "It's time to turn the tables and get some answers."

THE NEXT MORNING the sun was late in awakening as the sky was filled with clouds. The weatherman assured the viewing public that the clouds would linger but there was no chance of rain. However, the clouds seemed to disagree with his assessment as their dark hue signified that they could burst at any moment.

Donatella pulled her R8 Spyder in front of a nondescript apartment building near South Boulevard. Two teens, one black and the other white, eyed her as she parked against the curb.

The look in their eyes upon seeing the Spyder being driven by a woman gave them hope of an easy morning score. However, when they regarded the intense glare from Donatella's hazelnut brown eyes, they thought better of their life choices. Donatella, for her part, paid the two want-to-be thugs no mind, walking past them without a second glance.

The main entrance into the apartment complex was, at one point, guarded by a fence with a keypad entry. However, the keypad was gone leaving behind the pole that held it in place. The gate was no longer attached at the hinges. Instead, it lay up against the fence allowing easy access into the complex.

Agent Dabria walked through the complex aware of the eyes tracking her movements. For mere exercise, she contemplated how she could neutralize the foes she saw through her peripheral vision. She calculated that the time needed would be nine seconds and she would still have three bullets in her clip.

Ahead on left she spotted the numbers '528' slanted across the door. She approached, preparing to knock when the door was pulled open.

"Jesus Christ, get in here! Do you know how much your appearance here could mean trouble for me?"

"Hello Quinten," she said walking past him, conducting a quick survey of the room.

QUINTEN BALLARD, the former leader of the Q-Balls, was thin but built with sinew. He stood a shade over six feet with a shaved head and tattoos sprawled across his body. He was released two years ago after doing an eight year stretch for beating a rival gang member with brass knuckles for calling him a male Olive Oyl. It just so happened the gang member that he attacked had been working as an informant for the FBI and the assault took place two days before they were scheduled to make a major cocaine distribution bust.

For her part, Donatella kept tabs on Quinten while he was in prison. He would never come right out and admit it but going to prison likely saved his life.

Without his leadership, the Q-Balls membership floundered prior to splitting up to join other gangs just two years after his incarceration. Quinten who was no dummy, utilized his time behind bars to obtain his degree in sociology.

Upon his release, Donatella paid him a visit. She let him know in no uncertain terms that she would be keeping an eye on him, and if she found him straying down the wrong path, she would see to it that he was placed back behind bars.

In the two years since his release, she had only called on him once. She could tell he was uneasy about talking to her at the time and she assured him, she would only reach out to him if it was an emergency. And for Quinten Ballard, today was deemed an emergency.

"DONATELLA, you shouldn't be here. I could have met you somewhere other than where I have to lay my head."

He stopped talking to look at her. He forgot how truly stunning she was. Her smooth brown skin, jet black curly hair that rushed down to her shoulders. The black pant suit, that on anyone else would look ordinary, found the way to hug every curve she had in all the right places. Finally, it was her eyes. Those damn enchanting, hazelnut brown eyes. He recalled the Greek tale about the Siren's Lore realizing her eyes had the same affect.

She sat down not waiting to be invited, and Quinten followed suit. "I need some information."

"Well, damn. I figured that after the cryptic call last night followed by your appearance here today. You've had me up the whole damn night unable to sleep trying to figure out what trouble I would be getting myself into this time."

She raised an eyebrow but refused to take the bait. She knew he wanted to harp on the last time they met, but today she didn't have the energy to banter back and forth about the merits of their last encounter.

She pulled her phone from her pocket, "I'm looking for a woman by the name of Terri Buckley." She slid the phone over to him with Terri's picture filling the display.

"Come on, Donatella," he said in a pleading voice. "You know I'm not part of that life any longer. I'm doing everything I can to live the straight and narrow. Lord knows I don't want to end up behind bars again."

"That's good of you, Quinten, because I don't want to prove to you that I'm sincere about what I told you on your release. Nonetheless, I need you to inquire those that I may not be able to reach. I need you to keep your ear to the ground. I need you to check in with old acquaintances. I need to find this woman."

"Geez," he said mopping his forehead with the back of his hand. "What did she do to get on your bad side? Wait, it's probably better I don't know." He took another look at the picture on the screen. He had to admit that she was damn good looking too. Her eyes also stirred up feelings inside of Quinten; however, it was a dark sinister feeling that made the hair on the back of his neck stand up when he looked into them.

He shivered as if a gust of cold air had burst past him. Handing the phone back to Donatella he said, "I'll see what I can do, but you are putting me in an awkward position."

She took the phone from him, tapped a couple of buttons, and the phone next to Quinten began to vibrate. "I've sent you a copy of the picture. Quinten," she said, voice taking on a more dire and serious tone. "I want you to be extremely careful in this task. Terri is not someone you want to take lightly. I recommend you be as discreet as possible because you do not want to end up on her radar."

Quinten swallowed audibly, as she continued. "She is planning something that will likely affect countless people. She is not against dealing out death. In fact, she rather enjoys it. She is hidden underground, and I need to flush her out."

The silence lingered in the room for 10 seconds before Donatella abruptly stood. "If you find anything, call me." She walked to the door and prior to turning the knob she looked back and said, "Thank you."

18

T erri Buckley looked over her map of the city in conjunction with the plans she had in place. While her plan did not require everything to go perfectly for it to work, she wouldn't tolerate any subpar efforts from her team. Satisfied with the progress being made on that front, she turned her attention to her other special project.

She removed the map of the city from her desk and replaced it with building blueprints. The construction of the building was now complete. She had been part of the entire design process, but she continued to commit every part of the design to memory.

Francene walked into the room, a bottle of beer in hand. She sat in the metal chair across from where Buckley was standing with a quizzical expression across her face.

Buckley thought she was cute, but she was no Veronica King. Veronica had the presence, position, and raw sex appeal that Terri found becoming.

But as of late, she felt something was off with her. She

couldn't place her finger on exactly what it was, and she wondered if it meant she needed to watch her more closely.

Francene interrupted her thoughts, "So are you ever going to tell us what all this is for? I mean we've sworn a blood oath and we are in this until the end." She took a swig from her beer.

"You'll be off this train before it comes to an end," Terri said not taking her eyes off the blueprints.

"You know what I mean. We have put in so much work and it would be nice if we knew the final plan. Are you planning to make a political statement and take out government facilities?"

Terri stayed mute on the subject, so Francene decided to go down a different path. "Where did you learn all of, you know, the bad-ass skills? I've never witnessed anyone as polished as you are."

Again, Terri said nothing, eyes focused on her blueprints. Francene took the last swig of her beer, "Well, good talk. Let's do it again sometime." Recognizing Terri was not going to take the bait, Francene stood and left the office.

Buckley watched the woman leave the room, switching with each step. *I don't have time for distractions*, she thought looking back down to the papers on her desk.

Her focus was interrupted again, this time by her own thoughts. The appearance of Donatella at Veronica's house was bothersome. The fact Donatella was still sniffing around King meant she could not go back there, not until the agent was done for.

She then began looking around the warehouse. While it was next to impossible that Donatella could end up at this place, she needed to be prepared. She thought about it and then smiled, I know exactly what to do if, more like when, she shows up here. "I guess I better start planning for that as well."

ROBERT NOLAN DROVE off the lot of the Maserati of Charlotte dealership in his brand new Levante GranSport. He talked the dealer down to $85,000 cash out the door. He threatened to take his business, and his cash, elsewhere if they couldn't solidify a deal.

Understanding that money talks, he knew the salesperson would bend.

He connected his phone via Bluetooth, found "Beast Mode" by Ludacris and cranked up the volume. The car rode so smooth that if he wasn't rapping along to the music, it may have put him to sleep. He could hardly believe the job he had been on for the last few weeks. Several times he wished he had said no to the initial offer, but now, as he sat in his new ride, he was happy he saw it through.

With nothing better to do, and with the daylight fading, he figured he should go get a drink. He hadn't been to a bar in a while and Sully's was right around the corner. It was a trendy, posh bar with a better than average size parking lot. He figured it would be optimal as he didn't want any dings on his new whip.

He pressed repeat as the song neared its conclusion while he looked for a parking spot. He found one near the back of the lot with plenty of lighting. He pulled in, headfirst, placed the car in park and hopped out.

A voice from two cars over said, "Damn, Nolan. Is that your new ride?"

Without looking Nolan recognized the voice of Patricia Hill. She was top 10 in high school, but once you were introduced to women all around the county, her number continued to decline.

"Hey Pat," he said closing the door. "Yeah, it's mine. Just picked it up." "That's one sweet ride," she responded. "Maybe after you buy me a couple of drinks, you can take me for a ride in it."

While maybe not top 10 any longer, she was still a looker. "Sure thing, Pat. Let's go in and order a round or two."

They walked into the bar, wasting no time jumping into the booze. After 20 minutes and four shots later, Nolan found himself talking about the car and how he got the money for the car to a group of onlookers. Once he announced that rounds were on him, he had become everyone's friend.

"I'll tell you," he said throwing back his fifth shot and slamming the glass on the table, "the woman was crazy, sadistic. She had us do these jobs for her that still make no sense to me. But hey, she had a tight little ass and she paid well," he said taking another shot.

"Another round, barkeep," he said to the cheers from the crowd. Pat sat next to him the entire time, ensuring she would not lose her prize for the night. If he was throwing money around like this, he probably had some more at his house. With the speed he was drinking, he would likely pass out as soon as she got him back to his place. Even if he didn't, once she put it on him like she was known to do, he would fall asleep afterward.

Underneath the table she continued massaging his crotch to keep the idea at the front of his mind.

He completed his tale and after the seventh shot, announced that it was time to go. "Come on, Pat," he said as they stood up and he smacked her on the ass. "Let's go for this ride you were talking about earlier."

19

Sal woke up to three things he was no longer accustomed to since Jane moved into the apartment.

The first was the actual ringing of his alarm. For years he woke at 4 a.m. for a five- mile run. Although his running schedule had been momentarily interrupted, his body would not allow him to sleep beyond 6 a.m. Who was he kidding? Ever since Jane moved in with him his regular running session was replaced with a morning cuddling session.

Which brought him to point number two. Rolling over in the bed, he realized, more recalled, that he was sleeping alone last night. Jane, who trusted in superstitions, believed the bride should not see the groom on the day of the wedding prior to the official ceremony. He had become so used to having her in the bed next to him that he fought her decision to sleep at the Thompson's residence.

He tried telling her she wouldn't get any rest with a newborn in the house. Her response, "Who, Sebastian? That boy loves his Aunt Jane. He is like putty in my hands. He falls asleep, dead to the world, when I hold him to my bosom. It's almost like I was meant to have children."

At the mention of an offspring Sal was quick to change topics. Nonetheless, feeling the cool, unslept in, side of the bed that belonged to Jane felt somehow foreign to him.

The third thing was the butterflies rumbling around in his expanding gut. When Jane came back into his life, he was focused on a story about the missing kids within Driftwood Springs. His in-person encounter with her was the last thing he'd done before being kidnapped by that psychopath Terri Buckley.

The realization that he almost lost his life opened Sal's eyes. He knew Jane was the one for him and he made it his mission once everything settled down to have her in his life, prayerfully as his wife.

They grew closer during their reconnection and feeling out period. She convinced him to upgrade to a new dinette, forgoing the one he swore would be on this earth longer than him.

Now, as he lay in the bed, fully awake, with butterflies turning mercilessly in his stomach, he knew he had made the right decision.

"Sal, my man," he said aloud rising from the bed. "Today is the big day. You're about to marry the girl of your dreams. Don't mess it up."

As he bypassed the mirror leading into the bathroom he followed up with, "Get it together, Sal. You're packing on a few pounds."

And with that, Salvatore "Sal" Grandson made his way to the shower.

Marcellous sat in the nursery's rocking chair with Sebastian staring back at him, eyes full of the scenes that encompassed his world. The smell from Sebastian's latest blowout still lingered in the room even after disposing of it in the diaper genie.

"What did your mom feed you last night?" he asked only to be greeted with a devilish smile. Jasmyn was still breastfeeding, so he figured it had to be something she ate the previous night.

"The tikka masala," he said slapping his forehead with his free hand. *That certainly is not going back into the meal rotation until* Sebastian *is off the mommy milk regimen.*

Down the hall, he could hear the sounds of his wife helping Jane prepare for her big day. He flashed back on their ceremony and how gorgeous Jasmyn looked when the doors of the church swung open. In that moment, when their eyes connected, he knew he would do everything in his power to protect her and to give her the world.

He recalled how scared he had been when she was abducted by that crazy woman, Patti Jones, at the behest of Terri Buckley. Chasing the SUV that took her from the hospital racing across 277 to 77; he didn't know how he would save her. All he knew was he would save her and his unborn child. The thought made him squeeze Sebastian just a little tighter.

He looked down, "I'll never let anything happen to you either, my son." He kissed him on the forehead, receiving a giggle for his efforts.

"Marcellous, hun. Is everything ok? You need to get dressed; we'll be leaving soon."

He stood from the rocking chair, "Yeah, babe everything is fine. By the way, we need to talk about your Indian food craving from last night."

NANCY BREWER, the wife of Special Agent John Brewer, stood in the mirror, eyes misting over slightly. It had been nearly 10 years since she first brought up the topic of retirement to her husband. At the time, they still lived in Ohio and she thought there was a real possibility that she had convinced him.

Instead, John decided to take a promotion in Charlotte, North Carolina that had him leading the FBI field office. The fury that boiled under her skin when he announced his decision took months to get over. He knew how she felt about him accepting the position behind her back, one that meant they would need to uproot their lives.

They say love can endure all things, and it was her love for him that kept her by his side. Eight years later, she had to admit that it wasn't all bad.

She had him home for dinner more than she did when he was in the Ohio field office. His disposition changed to a much more cheerful one after they made the move. In part because of the exciting cases his team encountered, and ultimately solved. Not to mention, the amazing weather.

Unlike Ohio, and likely other portions of the Midwest, you didn't deal with gray skies from September to April. There was sun and lots of it. The temperature in the winter rarely dropped below 30, and when it did, it was only for a day or two.

Although there were some positives to their move south, Nancy was happy to see retirement at last. As a surprise, she had been squirreling away some of their disposable income for the last year. She saved enough to purchase them round-trip tickets to Hawaii where they would stay at a resort for seven days.

She planned to give him the surprise when they returned home, where she secretly hoped he would repay her with a little bedroom action. The thought brought a smile to her face. For now, she would bask in the knowledge that he was leaving behind the chaotic world of the FBI and that he would be safe by her side until they were old and gray. *Make that grayer,* she mused.

She left the bathroom, walking back into their bedroom. Upon seeing her husband, she couldn't help but to whistle, "Phwwwwwhhht, phwoooooh!"

Brewer turned around fussing with his tie. She continued, "Look at that handsome man there. Is it possible I can get your number?"

"Sorry, ma'am. I'm taken by a woman who would make us both disappear if she knew I was even looking at you."

"Lucky girl," she said, saddling up close to him. "But I'm sure she won't mind if I plant a kiss on your cheek." She leaned in, kissed him on the cheek, and then backed away with a smile.

"That's it, you've doomed us both now." They shared a laugh.

She moved his hands away from the tie, "After all these years, you would think you'd learn how to tie a knot correctly." She undid his effort, adjusted the lengths and began the Windsor knot motions she'd perfected over the years.

"Well, after today, I never plan to wear one again."

Nancy made the final adjustments and then slid it into place. She pulled the imaginary stray string from his white cotton shirt, "There, you're all set."

He kissed her on the forehead before turning around for his jacket. "You know," he said slipping it onto his arms and shoulders. "We should take a trip once all of this retirement business is out of the way. I wouldn't mind spending some time with my favorite girl."

She smiled, kissed him on the lips and asked, "How would your wife feel about you propositioning me like that?"

"I guess we better make sure she never finds out. Now come on, Mrs. Brewer.

Let's get this dog and pony show out of the way."

20

Special Agent Dabria was staring at nothing in particular when her cell phone rang.

Her eyes labored to regain focus as she pulled the phone from her pocket, *Quinten*. "Yes," she said in her familiar southern drawl.

"I might have something for you," he said in a semi-whisper.

Her eyes snapped into focus, and with a practiced urgency, "Proceed."

"Word on the street is Robert Nolan, a former member of my gang, has been driving around town in a brand new Maserati. I know him and his gang and they don't move enough product for him to afford a car like that."

Donatella sat a little straighter in her chair as her spine stiffened.

"I did some discreet checking and found out he was running his mouth at Sully's Bar. By all accounts he was drunk, and people for the most part blew him off. Anyway, he spoke of a job he pulled off for this sadistic, but gorgeous woman, who gave him the willies. He wouldn't go into the specifics of the job but did say she was camped out at a warehouse on the southside."

Donatella leapt from her chair and headed to the garage. "Thanks, I'll take it from here," she said disconnecting the call.

She retrieved her SIG Sauer P226, dropped it in the holster hugging her hip, and depressed the garage door opener. She determined speed would be of the essence, so she pulled her motorcycle helmet from its storage location in the garage and hopped on her Kawasaki ZX-6R motorcycle.

After strapping on her helmet, she shot out of the garage leaving the door to open the final few inches in her wake.

She raced through the community, catching stern looks from her neighbors, until she reached the gate. She downshifted to slow her momentum, turned the corner to the main street and opened the throttle.

She didn't know what she was going to do when she reached Terri, but the one thing she knew for sure was that she wasn't going to let her get away. From the corner of her eye, she noticed the walk sign ticking down toward zero as she approached the intersection. She picked up her speed in time to see the light turn yellow as she flew underneath it.

The scenery passed by in a mosaic of rapid colors, but her mind slowed down planning every action and reaction. She knew Terri would be the most formidable opponent she encountered thus far.

Eight minutes later, she skidded to a stop outside of the commercial warehouse building.

Donatella stepped off of the bike, removed her helmet, and began to survey her surroundings.

Although the warehouse was abandoned, there were telltale signs of activity. Tire tracks from a variety of vehicles could be seen entering and leaving the premises. A number of twigs from the bushes had been snapped. The dust that had accumulated on the stairs had been disturbed. Donatella knew this was the right place.

She placed her helmet on the back of the motorcycle while simultaneously pulling her SIG Sauer from its holster. Although there were no additional cars present, she wasn't taking any chances.

She climbed the stairs, one at a time, ears tuned for the slightest sound. The normal vibrations from a building when it's inhabited were missing thus giving additional credence to the building being empty.

At the top of the stairs, Donatella turned the handle on the outer door, unlocked. She cautiously pushed the door open, eyes scanning the entrance looking for any threats. Satisfied that the entrance was clear, she pushed her way in, all senses on high alert.

The inside was cavernous with moisture in the air and smelt of old takeout. Walking toward the center of the warehouse she could hear that faint buzz of an old TV set. She looked around, realizing the sound was not on this floor but instead coming from upstairs.

Every fiber in her being told her something was wrong, but her determination to bring this episode with Terri to an end drove her forward. She began her ascent to the top floor, eyes trained over her gun sights. Six steps from the top, a faint glow grew stronger while the buzzing sound grew louder.

At the top, she spotted an old floor model TV set plugged into an outlet with its back to her. Not willing to take anything for granted, she continued to clear her surroundings as she closed in on the TV. Movement caught her eye coming from the room on her left.

She swung her gun, eyes still over the sight, pressure applied to the trigger. The movement, a piece of debris, was carried across the floor by a gust of wind from an open window.

Donatella returned her focus on the TV while allowing her senses to concentrate on the remainder of her surroundings. Moving around the TV, she noticed a DVD player attached to the set with the remote sitting on top. Affixed to the remote was a note that read "Press Play".

The entire scene gave her a sick feeling in the pit of her stomach. Consciously aware of how unstable Terri had become, she knew nothing good would come from watching the video cued up in front of her. Nonetheless, she understood she had to proceed. She picked up the remote, pointed it at the TV, and pressed play.

Horizontal lines flashed across the blank blue screen as the DVD whirled around inside the disk player. After two seconds, maybe three, the face of Terri Buckley appeared on the screen.

"SPECIAL AGENT DABRIA, looks like we missed each other yet again," her voice taunted. "No doubt you've been wondering where I am, but you need not worry much longer as I'm sure we will be seeing each other real soon."

Involuntarily, Donatella looked around wondering if Terri was laying in wake somewhere she hadn't looked.

"You see, it's now time for us to play the game I promised you. As any athlete will tell you, when it's time for a big match, you cannot jump into the game without a proper warmup." A devious smile momentarily crossed her lips.

"So, to get your blood flowing, I've devised this warmup just for you. You know, you always thought you were the best, and to be honest I always hated you for that." Her eyes narrowed as the calm expression left her face, replaced with instantaneous rage.

Before she spoke again she visibly stilled herself, plastering the false indifference to her features.

"The other day, at least the other day from when I recorded this. No telling how long it's taken you to get here, but I digress. The other day I ran from this very spot to the exit in seven seconds. Maybe not my best performance, but good enough."

Again, the sadistic smile.

"I also calculated how long it took to record this video. Taking both pieces of information into account, and figuring you're supposed to be so much better than me –"

Donatella didn't wait for the remainder as she knew what was coming. She dropped the remote and began sprinting back toward the stairs. From behind her she could hear Terri's voice, "You have six seconds before this entire place goes boom!"

She hit the stairs at nearly top speed but slowed so she didn't topple going down. At the bottom, she picked up her speed again. If there was one thing about Terri, she was maniacal about her countdowns. If she said six seconds Donatella knew she had that and nothing more.

Her legs churned faster as she approached the door. In her mind she traced her steps back to entering the building. Had she pushed the door open or pulled the door open?

Pushed, she thought, realizing she would need an extra half second, something she was sure Terri didn't account for. In all likelihood, all doors were open when she made her seven second jaunt.

As she ran, she mentally rehearsed the steps needed to open the door, pick up speed again, jump on her motorcycle, and take off. She began to wonder if bypassing the bike and continuing to run was a better option. She'd make that decision as she drew closer.

The door was approaching fast, *time to act*. She reached out yanking open the door. Instead of running down the steps, she allowed her momentum to carry her as she jumped from the top straight to the bottom. She recalled that there were only five steps from when she counted them while when going up and she could clear the five without any problem. This would give her back the half second that she lost when opening the door.

The motorcycle was already facing away from the building as she always believed in wasting no time when needing to exit a location. And that one thing likely saved her life.

She hopped on the ZX, knocking the helmet off the back, and pressed the start button while simultaneously raising her feet to the pegs. Behind her she could hear the rumble of the building beginning to implode as the charges were detonating. She yanked the clutch and took off.

She could feel the heat from the explosion against her back as the motorcycle picked up speed. She felt her phone vibrate in her pocket. She pulled it out, "Private Number". She answered, keenly aware of who it would be.

"Good, you survived and are presumably warmed up, in more ways than one. Now, let the games begin."

21

Beep-beep. "Hurry up, dad. We're going to be late! Come on!"

"Just a second, Tyler. I'm talking to your mom."

"A lot of good that'll do," he mumbled under his breath. He started flipping through the radio station more from boredom than trying to find something to listen to. His attention was averted when he saw Lucy walking across the street.

Lucy Miller was the prettiest girl in school, at least that's what Tyler thought. He still hadn't worked up the courage to speak to her, but he was 60 percent of the way there. He knew she was out of his league, but he was determined to ask her to homecoming. He prayed she would say yes, but he was already planning on spending the night at home playing Call of Duty with his online friends. Friends he had never met but somehow, had more of a connection with than his so-called friends at school.

Look at her, he thought as she turned in his direction walking up the sidewalk. *She is perfect in every way.* As she passed by the car, he looked away not wanting their eyes to connect. He didn't want her to believe he was gawking at her. *I bet her hair smells good*, he thought picking her up in the side mirror as she cleared the car's bumper.

"See something you like?" his father asked, opening the door and sliding behind the wheel.

"Umm, well. She's alright."

"Sure, tell that to the drool pooling in the corner of your mouth." He quickly moved his hand to his mouth to wipe, nothing.

"Just go ahead and ask her out. The worst she can say is no. But I'm willing to bet she'll say yes."

"Oh, yeah?" he said with a sparkle in his eyes. "What makes you so sure? She's never given me the time of day."

As Peter pulled away from the curb he said, "Because I saw her glance in at you while you did the scared turtle trick. She had a smile on her face that said she found it cute."

"Cute?!" Tyler said blushing with embarrassment. "I will never live this down." His dad laughed, "It'll all be ok, but one thing for certain, she can't say yes if you never ask her. Now, what do you say we turn our attention to opening day? Panthers versus Bucs."

"Yeah!" Tyler exclaimed pumping his fist. "I think we have a good chance to take the division this year."

"I hope so. I'd love to have a home playoff game this year. I think I'll be able to score tickets this year if we make it."

"That would be so cool. Let's go Panthers, Let's Go!"

Peter smiled as opening day for the Panthers was at home this year and it fell on the weekend he had custody of Tyler.

He and Megan divorced a couple of years ago because of his drinking problem. He never laid his hands on her, nor was he bad with Tyler. The truth, he just wasn't a good guy to be around when he drank. For the sake of his family, he slowly began to put his life back together after spending time in A.A. and rehab. He was now sober for the last year and was gradually making his way back into her good graces.

He looked out the windshield into the sun shining from the sky, *nothing can ruin this day*, he thought.

———

ON THIS SUNDAY MORNING, Veronica King sat on the leather sofa curled up with her daughter. As the CEO of Global Insights Security, she rarely found time to rest and relax. But today, she cleared her calendar ensuring that the only thing on her plate was whatever Gina wanted to do.

They were preparing to watch a second episode of "Mickey Mouse Club House" when the doorbell rang. She wasn't expecting any visitors so she decided whomever it was could come back later.

10 seconds later the doorbell rang again.

"Mommy, someone is at the door," Gina said squirming in her arms. "I know, honey. They'll go away soon."

She could feel her daughter settle back in when her phone rang, "Private Number". "Veronica King," she said answering the phone with an irritated tone.

"Veronica, please open the door. We do not have all day."

She could tell from the curt tone that it was Lydia Brooks. She had not seen, nor heard, from the woman since her visit to The Syndicate headquarters.

"I'll be right back, dear," she said sliding from underneath her daughter. Several things ran through her mind about why Lydia was here. It certainly couldn't be anything to do with the company. If there was a problem, the company's officers would call her well before anything made it to the board. Which meant it could only have something to do with The Syndicate.

When she opened the door, Lydia stood there in a navy blue skirt, a blouse that was a shade of blush pink, and a matching navy blue jacket tailored to fit her figure.

Next to her stood a grandmotherly-type woman who looked to be in her mid-to-late 60s. She stood about 5-feet 2-inches tall with gray hair that was neatly styled and full of life.

"Veronica, I'd like you to meet Mildred. She is going to stay her with Gina while we take a ride."

Taken aback by the directness of the statement, she began to protest.

"I'll do no such thing! Today is the only day this week I have time to spend with my daughter and you will not interrupt it."

The woman smiled, "Ms. King, you took that statement as a request where in reality it was a command. Now, please introduce your daughter to her sitter, change into something more business appropriate and be prepared to leave in the next 10 minutes."

12 MINUTES later Veronica found herself in the back of the same town car as last time. Lydia once again rode with the windows smoked obscuring the scene outside.

Unlike the last trip to the undisclosed building, this trip didn't seem to take nearly as long. And also unlike the first trip, Lydia joined her as she entered the building.

The pair remained silent from the time Veronica came downstairs dressed and ready to go. But as they waited on the elevator, she couldn't hold her tongue any longer. "What exactly am I doing here and why couldn't this wait until tomorrow?"

"You are here because you were summoned, and you do not keep our host waiting.

Now if you can dispense with the questions, that would be great."

Veronica could feel her temperature rising, but she also knew there wasn't much she could do about it. She knew who they were and what they were capable of, so she decided to wait until the answer became apparent.

When they exited the elevator, she realized they were on a different floor from the last time she was there. The lobby, along with the receptionist, were not on this floor. Instead, across from the elevator stood a single, wooden door.

Lydia started in the direction of the door with Veronica following behind. As they approached the door, she saw a cutout on both sides of the door covered with glass.

Inside of each cutout was a beautiful blue flower. She couldn't recall the name of the flower and didn't have time to ponder it as Lydia opened the door continuing into the office area.

Upon entering the office space, the first thing Veronica realized was its massive size with wrap around floor-to-ceiling windows. Although the room was large, it was sparsely decorated. Because of the windows, the only location for personal objects was the wall adjacent to the door that they had entered.

With a click, the door closed behind them as they walked

toward the desk that sat three-quarters of the way into the room.

"Veronica, I'm happy you were able to join us today," came the voice from the woman she remembered as Ms. Blue. "Lydia, if you don't mind, I'd like to speak with Ms. King in private. I'll let you know when we have completed our conversation."

Lydia Brooks nodded her head, turned around and exited the door from which they entered.

Looking at the woman, Veronica had a strange feeling that her face was somehow familiar. Of course, she saw her when they met previously, but she swore she recognized the face outside of this setting. *Has this woman been following me on the streets,* she thought as her mind grasped for a memory.

"Come. Walk with me," she said standing from behind the desk, moving to a new location in the room.

Veronica did as she was requested, still wondering why she was here. "Look out of this window and tell me, what do you see?"

Veronica wondered if this was some type of trick question. She could attempt some complex, over-the-top answer but instead, she opted for a simple answer so that she could see where this was headed. "Well, I see the city."

The woman's eyebrow raised slightly as if she were questioning the answer. "The city," she said in a neutral tone. "Well, when I look out of this window, I see a chess board. Do you play chess, Ms. King?"

Veronica shook her head. "No, I don't," she replied in a curt voice wanting her to get to the point.

"I think it's something you need to learn as it's a fascinating game. In chess, there are a number of pieces that move around the board. You have your pawns, rooks, knights, kings, and queens. If I were to ask you, of those pieces, which one is the strongest on the board, what would your answer be?"

Again, feeling this was a trap and kicking herself for not knowing more about chess, she went with the obvious answer. "I would have to say the king is the strongest piece."

"Of course, you would. In a world dominated by men, the king would be the logical answer. But," she said turning to face Veronica, "the queen is the one who yields the most power on a chess board."

She turned back to face the window. "When I look out over the city, I see a lot of pawns. They are, by far, the most expendable pieces in a game of chess. You have people who run around willing to give their lives, if necessary, to win the game. It's true that some people do not realize they are pawns, and they contrive actions in a manner to elevate their station in life. But the reality is, they will always be pawns."

Veronica began to feel uneasy. Was this Ms. Blue trying to say that she was a pawn and by demanding answers from the leaders of The Syndicate she was contriving to move up? She began to protest, but decided it was probably best to listen.

"You previously inquired about how one moves up in our organization, so let me tell you a story."

"Many years ago, I was approached with the opportunity to ascend to the next station in my," she searched for the right word, "career here with The Syndicate. As with any organization, your performance and loyalty determine the next step in your career. It's no different here."

Veronica began to wonder what type of performance and

loyalty was needed to progress here. She realized the answer was likely on its way.

"I had met every requirement for the promotion, the only thing remaining was my act of no return." She paused, causing Veronica to look over at her. The woman's face hardened, and in that instance, she recognized why the face looked so familiar. *It can't be.*

Ms. Blue continued. "My act, the act that anyone who one day wants to sit in this seat must perform, was to terminate someone I held close to my heart."

Veronica's mouth hinged wide open, unsure if she heard the words correctly. "My act came on a day not too dissimilar from today. The weather was nice, the sun was shining, and many people did not realize that day would be their last day on earth. I watched as my," she paused again before continuing, "targets boarded their transportation for a business trip. The C-4 charges had been installed, per my design, and the detonator sat at my fingertips. It wasn't until later that I was informed that a secondary detonator had an override that would detonate the bombs even if I did not. As an organization, we couldn't risk someone spotting the charges."

Veronica almost moved her hand to her mouth understanding what was coming next. But she resisted the urge and continued to listen.

"When the target was safely aboard, I was given the greenlight to proceed. Without hesitation, I activated the detonator and watched from a helicopter as the yacht carrying my sister and her husband exploded into an unbelievably large fireball."

Veronica thought, *sister and husband!? Does that mean –*

Susan Yates continued, "With my act of no return

completed, I guaranteed myself the promotion and there was no turning back. This left my niece parentless, but I took her in and raised her until she became an adult. I also made sure she would be financially set for life."

The more the woman spoke, the more the pieces of the puzzle fell into place. This woman, who ran The Syndicate, was the aunt to Special Agent Donatella Dabria. She nearly asked to confirm her suspicions but decided she would hold onto that nugget of information. She would continue to pretend that she hadn't pieced the puzzle together.

"You see, Veronica," she continued, "as in the game of chess, when it comes to this city, the queen is the most powerful person, and make no doubt about it, I am the queen."

Veronica King stood thunderstruck not sure what to say or how to respond. The silence that filled the vast office space was suffocating.

After what felt like an eternity, Susan said, "I have brought you here today to witness a game of chess play out in real-time."

A knock came from the outer door and a smile creased her face. "At the door, Ms. King, is what we call in a game of chess 'checkmate'. Although the game is just about to start, those on the other end have already lost, and they just don't know it yet."

She turned to the door, "Enter."

22

P eter and Tyler made their way through the Panthers stadium in search of seats. Peter was thrilled that he was able to secure seats in section 114, the lower bowl. Although they were sitting on the visitor's side of the stadium, this was the closest they had ever sat to the field.

They stopped to ask one of the ushers to point them to their seats. She smiled a reassuring "I can help you with that" smile and led them to their seats.

Peter thanked her and Tyler said, "Dad, these seats are amazing." The look on his face was worth the price he had paid for the tickets.

He ruffled his son's hair, "Just wait until you see the cheer-leaders," he winked as they settled into their seats.

Tyler looked across the field and saw the huge bass drum making its appearance. This was one of his favorite traditions prior to kickoff.

Before each game the Panthers organization selected someone to "pound" the drum. The tradition came about from the heart and soul of their team, Sam Mills.

Mills was considered by NFL standards to be undersized for the linebacker position but he played with so much heart and determination that it became contagious throughout his team and the fans. He later became a coach for the team and his fiery attitude was carried onto the field by the players.

In August of 2005, he passed away at the age of 46 after fighting cancer for several years. The team took on the mantra, "Keep Pounding" as a tribute to their fallen star and beloved coach.

The mallet, as Tyler thought of it, was handed to a man in a Navy uniform. The crowd cheered as he swung back and with each pound of the drum they chanted in unison, "Keep Pounding", "Keep Pounding". Tyler yelled at the top of his lungs with each successive strike of the drum.

Finally, the teams were introduced, the away team followed by the home team.

They were so close to the field, when the fire shot up from the entrance onto the field for the Panthers' players, he could feel the heat on his skin.

The beer guy was climbing the steps when the patron sitting next to Peter signaled for a beer. The money was passed down the aisle and the beer was returned. Peter could smell the hops as the beer got closer and by the time it reached his hand, he was salivating. He passed it along, willing himself to block it out of his mind.

The Panthers won the coin toss and decided to receive, a rarity in today's NFL game. Typically, teams wanted to kickoff to start the game so that they would receive the opening kickoff in the second half. As it turned out, the decision to receive the kickoff was the right decision.

The returner took the ball one-yard deep in the end zone

and then ran up the middle before diverting to the right side where he raced up the sideline untouched for a 101-yard opening kickoff touchdown. The team was in a frenzy, Peter and Tyler, who had jumped out of their seats during the runback, exchanged high-fives, and for the second time that day Peter thought, *nothing can ruin this day.*

SALVATORE "SAL" Grandson pulled his 2002 Honda Accord into the closest parking spot to the courthouse. For a minute he considered taking the spot furthest away so that he could get in some additional steps but then thought better of it. Jane would likely want to hop right into the car and head home for the reception.

Marcellous, the best man, pulled into the parking spot next to Sal. When he hopped out of the car he said, "Sal, my man. The day is finally here." He was smiling ear-to-ear upon making this statement and Sal couldn't help but to smile in return.

"Hey, Marcellous," he said sticking out his hand.

Marcellous pushed off the handshake, "Come on in here, you big lug," he said pulling the older man in for an embrace. Sal returned the hug, butterflies still bouncing around in his stomach.

"Did you happen to see Jane this morning?" he asked, shielding his eyes from the sunlight.

"Yes, I did. Jasmyn was putting the finishing touches on her makeup. She's gorgeous, Sal. You picked a winner." Marcellous patted him on the back.

"I think we better get in; the ladies were right behind me."

"Good thinking," he said as they walked up the stairs leading into the courthouse. "Say, how do you like the ride in your Tesla?"

"I absolutely love it. Minimum cabin noise, smooth acceleration and not smelling the fumes from the gas station is the best."

"I've been thinking about splurging on one for myself. Maybe after we return from the honeymoon I'll stop by the service center and take one for a spin."

"It'll change your life. You'll never want to go back. Looks like the minister is standing right over there. We should go."

The pair made their way over to the minister who grinned on their approach. "Sal," he said extending his hand, "today's the big day."

Sal took the proffered hand, "Yeah, I can't wait to get this underway. Hopefully I can make it to the end without making a fool of myself."

"No worries, I'll take good care of you," the minister said. "And I'm sure Marcellous here will catch you should you faint."

Sal realized he hadn't thought about fainting. Now that it had been mentioned, it was stuck in his head.

"Let's head in and get you situated. Is the blushing bride here as well?"

Marcellous took this question, "Jasmyn and Jane are only a few minutes behind us. They should be here shortly."

"Perfect." The minister led them through a series of hallways that ended at courtroom number three. He walked Sal and Marcellous through where they would stand and then asked, "Do you plan to recite your own vows or will you go with the standard wedding vows?"

"I plan to recite my own." Sal spent most of his life writing for one reason or another, so writing his own vows gave him a sense of comfort.

The minister nodded in agreement, "Well, the only thing we need now is the guest of honor.

As if hearing the words directly from his lips, Jasmyn Thompson came walking into the courtroom. In the baby carrier, Sebastian slept unaware of the momentous event he was about to experience.

Marcellous watched as his wife walked toward them. He always thought she was gorgeous, but today she reached a new level of radiance emanating from her aura. He stepped away from Sal who wiped a bead of sweat that began to form on his forehead.

"Here, let me take him," Marcellous said upon reaching his wife. After his blow out earlier that morning, his outfit had to be changed. Marcellous thought the outfit he picked out for his little man made him look dashing; however, Jasmyn didn't agree. She told him to head on over to the church and she would find him a new outfit. When he looked into the carrier, he had to admit the outfit she chose was better suited for the occasion than the one he had selected.

Jasmyn handed him the carrier and leaned in to kiss him on the cheek. After pulling away she asked, "Have you seen Donatella?"

He had to admit that he hadn't even thought about the FBI agent. "No, I haven't seen her. Maybe she is running a little late."

"You think? The bride is right outside the door, ready to walk in. We can give her another minute or two at most, but then we will need to get started."

They both looked back at the door and a shared thought crossed their minds, *I hope everything is ok.*

DONATELLA'S GRIP on her phone tightened while she worked to bring her breathing back under control.

"Cat got your tongue?" Terri mocked. "Let me provide you some details to our game. I told you when I had your precious goddaughter and that useless reporter, Sal Grandson, that you could not save them both. But once again, Special Agent Donatella Dabria to the rescue and they are both walking this earth today."

Donatella's mind raced, *could she be going after Bree?* She had a sick feeling as she knew there wasn't anything she could do if Terri had an attack planned on Bree at this moment.

"Today, you choose. Your friends or some strangers. I warned you that I had a few people I needed to payback. Smithville was first, that worthless piece of shit. It felt good to hear him scream as I had done for years because of what he did to me. Now, onto phase two."

"What delusional drivel are you spewing, Buckley?"

"Drivel," she laughed. "You have some nerve, but I guess that's a good place to start. The journalist, Grandson, depicted me as a monster that needed to be hunted down. A monster!" she yelled.

"Since he decided to assassinate my character, I decided to let the monster out to play. With today figuring to be the happiest day of his life, I decided to give him an explosive gift.

I have to admit, even though that Jane woman he is preparing to marry is a tad older, she ain't too bad looking."

Donatella snapped out of the verbal trance, dropped the wireless earbud into her ear, and began moving toward the courthouse.

"As a bonus, I hear that Marcellous Thompson will be in attendance. Having him and Sal in the same place at the same time lessened the risk I needed to account for during the planning process. Now before you go off halfcocked ready to save the world, I should inform you about one other crucial piece of information."

Donatella shifted to the next gear picking up speed. *What the hell is she talking about?*

"For someone who prefers to work alone, you brought a lot of assistance to our last confrontation. I'm not sure who you have behind the scenes working the technical magic, but I have something for him or her as well."

BJ, she thought quickly. *How on earth does she plan to get at BJ?*

"I've had both the courthouse and the Panthers stadium wired with explosives. Not only are they wired, but they are also interconnected. I've added my own brand of security to both locations. Let's just say communication in and out of both places will be impossible. Not to mention, I've retrofitted each location with new on-premises security."

"Terri, there's tens of thousands of people at that stadium. You cannot be serious!" The panic and stress could be heard in her voice.

"I'm deadly serious. Now make sure you don't go off and get yourself killed, because you and I have a date once all of this is done." The phone went dead.

Donatella, understanding that there was no time to waste, placed a call to BJ.

"My favorite FBI Agent, how –"

"Bryce," she shouted with urgency dripping from her lips. "I need you to concentrate as we do not have much time."

BJ knew Special Agent Dabria to be a cool customer. Her tone snapped him into focus, "What can I do?"

"Terri has rigged explosives at the courthouse where Sal and Jane are having their wedding. She has also managed to set explosives at Bank of America Stadium, the home of the Panthers. I'm headed to the courthouse to stop the bomb. I need for you to take care of the explosives at the stadium."

BJ felt his mouth go dry.

"She mentioned that the communication in and out of the stadium has somehow been jammed; however, she also mentioned that the bombs are linked."

BJ interrupted, "They must have created some sort of private network that they are operating from."

"My thoughts exactly. See if you can break through the network and stop the bomb at the stadium. My focus will be the courthouse. BJ," she said stressing his name, "We have to stop them."

"I'm on it. I'll be in touch." He disconnected the call, a first in their relationship.

Normally, Donatella was the one to disconnect.

FIVE MINUTES LATER, Donatella pulled into the parking lot of the courthouse. She saw the vehicles belonging to Sal, Marcellous, and Jasmyn. She hoped off of the ZX letting the bike fall to the ground as she bound up the steps.

She burst through the outer doors in search of courtroom number three. Upon locating the room, she was horrified at what she saw.

A second set of steel doors had been closed and locked into place outside of the courtroom. She realized this is likely what Terri meant about additional on-premises security. She had, effectively, trapped the wedding party inside the room as if it was a prison.

She thought about banging on the door and then realized that would do her no good. Even if the wedding party heard her, they couldn't escape. The only thing she could do was locate the bomb and then find a way to disarm it.

The most logical location would be in a room next to the ceremony. However, from everything she knew about Terri, she knew her plans were not subtle. Taking out a room or two would not be part of the plan. If there was a bomb in this building, it made sense that the entire building would be the target.

She looked around, located the sign for the stairwell, and raced off.

THE EXCHANGE with Donatella freaked him out. On several occasions, BJ was part of a high-stakes plan where lives were in danger. However, this was the first time that tens of thousands of lives hung in the balance.

She didn't exactly give him much to work with, but he had been given much less in the past and managed to perform miracles. Furthermore, after all she had done for him, he wouldn't let her down.

.   .   .

BRYCE JACOBS and Donatella crossed paths when he was being investigated for creating a method to predict winning numbers for the lottery. He did it merely as an academic exercise and had not profited from his creation. Because of that, Donatella managed to get him probation and he worked with her on special projects every now and then.

Working on these side projects with Donatella brought clarity and definition to his life. It brought him a sense of purpose and belonging. For those reasons, he had never failed her.

FIRST THINGS FIRST, he had to locate the private network that The Syndicate was working from. Finding that network would give him eyes into what they had set up.

BJ figured The Syndicate would not broadcast over your typical business or personal internet service providers like Spectrum or AT&T. Any work performed on one of the major companies networks could be traced. Sure, they could eliminate their activity later, but it wasn't worth the risk.

The other reason is that they would lose control over the network. Terri made it clear that she wanted Special Agent Dabria to know what she was up to. If they were on a public network, the provider could simply cut the access. For those reasons, he knew they were operating on a private network.

Upon conducting this initial search, he was left with 122 contenders. The next filter would be those on a private network that was transmitting a large amount of data. It's true that a number of people are hyper-sensitive about their personal data and thus they always work from their own private VPN. However, they typically weren't transmitting the amount of data BJ felt was necessary for what The Syndicate was trying to accomplish. This filter left him with five viable contenders.

While VPNs provided a level of encryption, the level needed for this act of terror would not be your garden-variety VPN. He figured additional layers of security would be added to keep them hidden as long as possible.

"Two possibilities," he said out loud.

He immediately set multiple computers on the task to break the encryptions. The computing power in his setup would rival the world's most powerful super computers. So, breaking this encryption should be a cinch, nonetheless he willed them along to run faster.

After 15 seconds he had access into the first computer. In looking through the file structures and the data being passed, he realized it was illegal porn. He immediately dismissed it and waited for the second to finish.

That one finished 40 seconds later. He stilled himself for the challenge ahead, when to his dismay it looked to be electronic currency being transferred.

"Shit, did I make the wrong assumptions?" He mentally traced through his rationale again and it all seemed solid. "Think, BJ. Think," he banged his fist on the table. "What am I missing?"

Then it hit him. He dismissed the porn site without really looking into it. He went back to the computer and scrutinized what was there. It took him a few minutes but there it was. Network packets running as a sub process behind the porn.

"Damn it! I cannot believe I wasted that much time."

He immediately began deciphering what he was looking at when he realized this was the security for the stadium. His eyes raced over the programming logic when he noticed that the program controlled the electronic gates at the stadium entrances.

Since finding the explosives was his primary task, BJ set a tickler on the section of code that would control the gates.

A tickler is a particular program meant to perform a task. BJ had a number of them at his disposal. This particular tickler would immediately grab his attention.

If he had more time, he would have manipulated the code so that the gates would function only when he deemed it necessary; however, time was at a premium.

It took him a shade over a minute, but he finally located the first explosive. If the situation wasn't life or death, he would have patted himself on the back, instead he immediately started the trace routine that would locate the remaining bombs.

At that moment, the proximity sensors activated from his computer. He turned to his second monitor where he determined someone was attempting to hack into his system.

"Not now," he said. He had two additional fail safes that the intruder would need to bypass before he would need to take action. On one previous occasion, someone managed to crack through the first layer, but no one had ever cracked the second layer.

As he turned his chair to follow the trace, the second alarm chimed.

"Already?! Impossible." The first time someone penetrated beyond his first layer of defense, it took them three hours. This hacker did it in a matter of seconds.

He let the trace run in the background and diverted his focus to the attack. It only took him a glance to realize the hacker was utilizing the same private network that the bombs were connected to.

He opened a command prompt and got to work fortifying his defenses. Whoever it was worked quickly and efficiently. They were already 30 percent of the way through his second layer.

In the midst of throwing up an impromptu roadblock, a message appeared on his screen.

"Hello Bryce. You are messing in matters that do not concern you. Stop while you are ahead or I will destroy your precious setup."

Taking the bait, he responded, "Who is this?"

"It doesn't matter who this is. Stop or be destroyed."

"I don't think so," he said with more conviction than he felt. This person was likely a psycho. At best they worked for a psychotic organization.

"Don't say I didn't warn you."

The chat window died and BJ watched as the intruder was at 45 percent of the way through his defense. Although he had the third and final layer, at this rate the intruder would be through the second layer in a matter of minutes.

He hastily cobbled together some additional security methods. He didn't expect them to stop the intruder, just merely meant to keep them occupied so that he could deal with –

Alarms began blaring from the speaker on his computer. It was the tickler. He turned back to the monitor that was running the trace on the bombs. It was still working, only three had been found.

The tickler informed him that the gates were being lowered at all of the entrances. He composed himself, realizing that he was fighting three different battles at once. Finding the bombs, dealing with the gate that would trap people inside the stadium, and the mad-hacker attacking his private setup.

He prioritized the work. His private setup could be restored. He had everything stored in the cloud so no harm, other than to his ego. People being trapped in the stadium wouldn't be a problem as long as he could find the bombs. So, the bombs became the priority.

As he turned his attention back to the bombs, the first bomb in the chain went offline. A sick feeling in his gut told him that the bomb had just detonated. And he was right.

23

"Wow, what a quarter," Tyler said to his dad. "Not only did they return the opening kickoff for a touchdown but they also had two sacks, and the Bucs cannot stop the Panthers running attack."

"And just think," Peter picked up, "there's still three more quarters to dominate these scrubs."

Tyler laughed as they scurried to the concession stand in search of refreshments. Peter looked at his phone for the fourth time that afternoon. Tyler noticed this and said, "Waiting on a call?"

"Well, no," he responded. "For some reason I'm not receiving any service, which is weird because I don't recall falling behind on the bill."

Tyler who considered himself to be the next Steve Jobs said, "Here, let me see it."

Peter looked at him sideway, but nonetheless handed over the phone. After a few minutes Tyler said, "Yep, looks like you don't have any service."

"Well, thank you genius. I would have never figured that out without your assistance."

"I'm always here to assist the elderly."

"Why you –" Peter said as he gave a mock chase after his son.

A minute later, as they stood in the concession line, Tyler turned to his father and asked, "Why did you and mom breakup? I mean she never talks about it, you never talk about it, so it makes me wonder what happened."

Peter, not expecting the question, tried to find a way to articulate that he was an alcoholic that didn't deserve a second chance with the best woman he ever dated. He then said, "Did you feel that?"

A wry smile touched Tyler's lips, "Ha-ha, Dad. Don't try to weasel out of answering my question. I think I'm old enough –"

The words caught in his throat as they both heard and felt the stadium shake. From a distance, they both thought they heard what sounded like screams.

Peter's survival and parental skills took over, "Come with me, Tyler." His tone left no room for interpretation. They both stepped out of line, Peter leading the way.

A loud, "boom" was followed by the stadium shaking and screams cascading. "Run!" Peter said to his son and they took off. Their lower-level seats meant that they were closer to the exit and they made a straight line, along with some others who realized something was seriously wrong, to the exit. When they arrived, to their dismay, they saw that the gates were closed preventing them from exiting the stadium.

"This way!" Peter yelled, dragging his son through the

crowd, eyes searching for another exit. He could feel the panic building in his chest as he heard another "boom".

Similar to the previous sounds, the stadium shook. This time however, both the sound and the stadium vibrations felt closer.

The fans that were still in their seats began rushing out into the concourse.

Peter spotted another exit sign. He shoved, pushed, and maneuvered his way through the frantic crowd. He could feel Tyler's grip tight on his own. He would not let his son's hand go for any reason. When they arrived at the second gate, he damn near lost it. That gate was closed as well.

His mind began to process the scene. The loud sounds, the stadium vibrations, the hysterical fans, and the locked gates. This could only mean one thing, *a terrorist attack*. He looked around again realizing that they were trapped on the inside.

His mind raced, *there had to be another way out of here.*

"Dad!" he heard his son yell over the crowd, "What's going on? How do we get out of here?"

In response to the questions, Peter snapped out of his trance and began looking for another gate. As they continued on their path in the concourse, Peter looked through the opening at the other side of the stadium. In place of the bleacher, that a moment ago was filled with fans screaming on the success of the Panthers, he now only saw black smoke and an open sky.

He pulled Tyler with a renewed urgency when he heard the myriad of sounds once again. He nearly tripped over a man who had been trampled but managed to keep his balance. He knew it was only a matter of time, but still he ran, moving through the mass of humanity, in search of an exit.

He spotted the sign he was in search of, *third one has to be the charm*, he told himself. He could see fans being crushed up against the gate, as the crowd tried desperately to escape the fate that they all knew was headed their way. In a moment of calm, he stopped. He pulled his son to him, holding him in a tight embrace. Into Tyler's hair he simply said, "I love you, son."

ROUGHLY 20 SECONDS after the first bomb in the chain disappeared from BJ's screen, the second one disappeared. The trace he was running had not completed and he didn't have a full account of what he was dealing with at that moment, and to be honest, it didn't matter.

If the bombs were going off, it was too late to run a trace to disconnect them. He was dealing with an unspecified number of explosives, so he needed to pivot to Plan B. He focused his attention, once again, on the gates holding the patrons inside of the stadium.

His fingers were gliding with precision over the keyboard feverishly stroking the keys. The speed at which he was typing gave his fingers the sensation of growing colder. Both his mind and his fingers worked in unison. If he could override the program, he would have control over the gates.

He heard another chime. He didn't need to look over to know what that meant. The hacker was now 90 percent of the way through his second layer of security. He paid it no mind and continued to work.

A message appeared on his screen, "I warned you to stop while you were ahead. You didn't listen. It'll only get worse from here."

BJ ignored the statement, pushing his brain to the limit.

"I can put an end to all of this, all you need to do is say four little words 'I'm better than you.'"

The wise-ass in BJ thought about the statement and decided, *I am better than you*, though he knew what the hacker meant. But this was no time to piss them off. He wouldn't dignify their demand with a response. Instead, he typed faster.

In that split second, he made a calculated risk and changed his mind. He typed back, "You are right, I am better than you" and hit send.

He pushed his fingers as fast as they would go.

"Bryce Jacobs, you think you are so smart. Well, good luck sleeping with the death of the entire stadium on your conscious."

Again, he ignored the comment, calculating on what would come next. As expected, the code on his screen began to disappear from in front of his eyes. He said a quick prayer hoping his gamble would pay off.

The gamble came in the form of a piece of logic he saw during his first pass of the code. While his initial attempt was to gain control over the gates, he realized that the hacker put a safety measure in place that would destroy the program on command. The intent was to ensure that no one could gain access to the gates and thus opening them.

On the fly, he wrote a program that would set the gates back to the factory setting should the "self-destruct" code be enabled. The factory setting would likely have the gates in an open position.

BACK AT THE STADIUM, ANOTHER "BOOM" went off growing ever so close to Peter. He squeezed his son, who squeezed him back.

At that moment he heard the rattling. He opened his eyes to see that the gate was, indeed, moving. Without warning, he released the embrace of his son and began moving forward.

Tyler was startled at first but soon, he too, realized that the gate was moving. He grappled for his dad's hand, missed, and then grabbed again. They were moving to the front quickly. They could see the exit, a mere 10 yards away, when they heard another boom.

A fissure grew diagonally from the base of the wall next to them toward the ceiling. Peter tugged harder willing Tyler to move faster. Pieces of concrete began to chip away from the ceiling, falling on the fleeing fans.

Peter exploded through the gate where the bottleneck opened up to the free air outside of the stadium.

He turned around, prepared to hug Tyler, when his heart sunk. The person he had been leading out of the building was not Tyler, it was some other little boy he had never seen before.

In a panic he turned around and began yelling his son's name. In the noise and confusion, he thought he heard, "Dad, in here."

He raced back to the entrance pushing his way through the crowd doing their best to exit the stadium. That's when he noticed Tyler, still inside the stadium another 10 yards from the exit. The rush of people jostled him backward as they shoved and pushed each other in search of freedom.

He pushed his way back to the entrance but was being swept away by the sheer number of people exiting. Again, he heard, "Dad, in here." His watched helplessly as his son tried in vain to pull himself forward.

He screamed out, "Tyler, I'm coming. Tyler –"

His voice was drowned out by another loud "boom". He could see his son and his son now saw him. Their eyes locked before Peter saw the concrete collapse at the entrance.

24

D onatella rushed down the stairwell aiming for the basement. This was the logical location for any explosives Terri would have stored within the building. She racked her brain formulating a plan once she reached the bomb.

As part of their FBI training, her class was afforded the opportunity to train alongside the bomb disposal unit. Unlike her focus to detail in hand-to-hand combat and weapons training, Donatella gave bomb disposal only a passing glance. She found the men and women that signed up for this particular job to be fascinating. Although it wasn't something she could see doing herself, she respected those who chose it as a career.

When she reached the ground floor, she thought about how much more comfortable she would feel if she had paid better attention. Or better yet, if she had access to one of the bomb disposal robots.

Entry into the section of the basement that she needed to

access was locked. To enter, she would need a keycard with the appropriate access. Unable to provide the required card, she pulled her SIG Sauer from its holster, racked a bullet into the chamber, and fired into the magnetic lock located above the door. She yanked the door open and continued her search through the basement.

She prayed that BJ was succeeding with the crisis at the stadium. For now, her focus was on the courthouse and he would need to deal with the stadium.

Donatella surveyed the basement, *where would someone place a bomb if they were trying to bring down the building?"* She looked around frantically for 20 seconds when it hit her, *a load bearing wall.*

While she wasn't an architect, she recalled reading some-where that all buildings had at minimum one wall or struc-ture meant to distribute the weight of the building. She focused her search on columns running perpendicular to the floor. After a moment, she spotted the first one. She ran over to the column, circled around, nothing.

Her eyes went back to scanning the basement when she located a second one. As she drew closer to the column, she heard a faint hum. She circled the column and there, in front of her, sat the bomb. Blocks of C-4, wires running into a box connected to the C-4, and wires running to a contraption attached to a tablet. A green light sat atop the box giving off an ominous glow.

She activated the tablet expecting to see a countdown timer, but instead she was greeted with a normal looking home screen. If it wasn't for the severity of the situation, she would have found this humorous. What better way to disguise the controls than by simply leaving everything as is on an out-of-the-box tablet.

She decided to try the obvious. She opened up the settings application looking for anything that screamed bomb controls. To her dismay, but still not surprised, she didn't find anything. Next, she scrolled through all of the apps, and again, nothing stood out.

Although there wasn't a clock ticking down the time second by second on the tablet, she could feel the time slipping through her fingers.

She thought about destroying the tablet, but she knew in doing so, it would likely set off the bomb.

She closed her eyes while taking in a deep breath. She slowly released the air pondering her next steps as the air left her lungs. A thought popped into her mind.

She pulled up the search for the tablet and put in her name, "Donatella".

An app, hidden from public view, was returned as part of her search. She opened the app and was greeted with the mapping of the wires to the C-4, similar to the display when setting up a Nest home thermostat. Idly, she thought, *guess this is the new age equivalent to cutting the wire.*

As she stared at the diagram, she willed the knowledge of bomb disposal to come flooding back. Then she decided that there was no time to lament, only time for action.

MARCELLOUS LOOKED DOWN at his watch to check the time realizing Donatella would officially miss the wedding. *That's odd, I don't have any service,* he idly thought when he checked the watch face. When the doors opened, he lost his thought. Jane stood at the entrance, simply glowing. As she walked down through the door there was no mistake, she was gorgeous. The tough Sal Grandson would never admit to it, but Marcellous was 95 percent sure that he saw a tear form in the corner of his eye, make that 99 percent.

Sal watched every step Jane took as she made her way to the altar. When she arrived he said, "You look amazing."

Jane smiled and said, "You clean up pretty darn well yourself." The love that radiated from the two of them was infectious.

With the wedding party fully assembled, the minister started. "Ladies and gentlemen, we are gathered here today to witness the marriage of Salvatore Arthur Grandson and Jane Alice Markowitz. Marriage is a union of two people who love each other unconditionally, and their love is something that no man or woman can tear asunder. I understand that the bride and groom have written their own vows. Jane, please recite your vows to Sal."

"Sal, I have loved you from the moment we first met. That sunny day in May, we were competing journalist on the Ludlow case. I never told you then, but watching you work the police for information was pure genius. From that moment on, every time I saw you my heart would skip a beat, multiple beats.

As I stand here today, ready to say I do, I am once again reminded of how much I love you. How much I want to grow old with you. How I want to be the woman to care for you through sickness and in heath, for better or for worse.

Sal, the song says you're the wind beneath my wings, but

for me, you're the air within my lungs. I vow I will love you, as I have always loved you, until the day I die."

She turned back to the minister, signaling that she was done. He, in turn, shifted and said, "Sal, your vows."

Sal stood at the altar, mouth parched and a tear streaming down his cheek. All the words that he had written escaped his brain as he looked into Jane's beautiful, sparkling eyes. The only words he could muster were, "Oh Janie, I do!"

The minister said, "Sal, we haven't quite gotten to that part yet."

Sal managed to pull himself together and provided an abbreviated version of the vows he had written. The minister completed the perfunctory ceremony and then concluded. "Sal and Jane, I now pronounce you husband and wife. You may kiss the bride."

Sal pulled Jane in closer, kissing her with the passion he felt in his heart.

"Ladies and gentlemen, let me introduce to you, Mr. and Mrs. Salvatore Grandson."

Marcellous and Jasmyn cheered as the couple stepped down from the altar. Their smiles became infectious to the point that the Thompsons found themselves grinning from ear-to-ear. This all came to an end when the PA came to life.

"Let me be the first to congratulate the bride and groom," the unseen voice crackled. "It's a shame that I couldn't be there to give my regards in person."

The hairs on the back of Sal's neck stood straight up. He recognized the voice but was having a hard time placing it. When she began to speak again, there was no doubt in his mind who was behind that voice, Terri Buckley. His heart rate rapidly increased.

"Sal, it's been so long since we spoke. And looky here, you've met a nice woman to share your last moments on earth with."

"Sal, who is this woman?" Jane said in a panic. "What is she talking about?" Terri stepped on Sal's chance to respond, "Then we have Marcellous and Jasmyn Thompson. I must say, Jasmyn, post pregnancy has done you well. My God, you are a gorgeous woman."

Marcellous and Jasmyn looked at each other with Jasmyn feeling the need to subconsciously cover herself.

"But enough of the small talk. Let's get down to business. Sal, you've had some, let's say rude and crude things to say about me in your articles. Defamation of character, if you will. Most of it I passed off as a way to grab more readers. But," she said, menace in her voice, "You crossed the line when you called me a monster. That was pushing it a little too far."

Jane, who had read all of Sal's article recalled the article in question. It took her only a moment to pull the name from her memory.

"Terri Buckley," she said, more in a question than a comment. "You're sick. You're beyond sick. You are a twisted, vile individual. How dare you interrupt my day. Sal was right, you are a monster, and you should be thrown in jail from everything I've heard. You get off on torture and mayhem, it's clear you need some help. Some serious fucking help!"

Sal placed a hand on his wife's shoulder in an effort to calm her. He knew how she could get when she was riled up.

"You sure know how to pick them, Sal. She's a feisty one. But I must move on, because you all are running out of time. Now to you, Mr. Thompson."

"You are also the reason I'm here today. You see, had you not stuck your nose where it didn't belong, I would have left the city of Charlotte. I would have had no other reason to stay. But when you saved Donatella at the Cleveland Museum of Art, I had to stick around. It's not only imperative that she die, but she must also do so by my hands."

Marcellous was done listening to this psycho, "Come on guys, let's go." The group began walking toward the doors at the back.

"Yes, you are the take charge kind of guy. Good for you, but I'm afraid you will not be going anywhere."

When Marcellous pulled the doors open, he saw a set of metal doors that were not there when they arrived.

"You see, today, I'm righting some wrongs in my life. Sal, Marcellous, you two happen to be on the list. Fear not, your demise will be swift. But alas, I have more I need to accomplish before this day is done. Enjoy your last few precious moments together, and once again, congratulations on your wedding. You are a beautiful bride, Jane."

With that, she was off. Marcellous, Sal, and the minister tried moving the door. It wouldn't budge. Jasmyn pulled out her cellphone to dial 911. When she placed the phone to her ear, all she heard was silence.

Confused, she looked back down at her phone, "I don't have a signal."

Marcellous checked his phone, again, "Me either. She must be blocking it somehow."

There were no windows in the courtroom, so they began banging on the door. But there was no one within earshot to hear their pleas.

NEXT TO EACH wire detailed on the tablet was a lever. The lever appeared to denote if electricity flowed from the tablet to the detonation box. While each wire had a lever, every lever had not been set to send an electrical charge.

Instantly, she began to wonder, *are some of the wires decoys? Or could activating some of the wires be the key to shutting down the device?*

The voice in the back of her head reminded her of the nonexistent countdown clock that steadily ticked away. She began to analyze the configuration.

Two black wires ran parallel to each other from the laptop into the box. Only one of the black wires was active. Three green wires were running in an alternating fashion with yellow, blue, and finally red. Two of the green wires were active along with the blue and the red. Finally, a random fuchsia color ran diagonally across the wires and it too was active.

She recalled that all explosive ordinances have a ground wire. She couldn't recall if the ground wire was a good thing or a bad thing. She also knew that a wire would allow the explosive to be deactivated.

By process of elimination, the wire that allowed the bomb to be deactivated must be one of the wires that had electricity flowing through it.

The imaginary running clock nagged at her subconscious. The bomb could go off at any minute killing her and her closest friends.

She decided to discount the black wires as the ground

wires. Traditionally, black acted as the ground. That left the two green, the blue, the red, and the fuchsia wires.

For no reason other than the fact that movies always have the red wire as the one you don't want to cut, she ignored that one.

She then discounted the two green wires. She figured Terri didn't set the explosive therefore she wouldn't want it to inadvertently detonate.

Her mind raced between the blue and the fuchsia. The latter she started to think of as a trojan horse. The fact that it ran diagonally across the bomb's structure was troubling.

As flawed as the logic may have been, her mind kept going back to blue and the color continued to emerge as the answer.

She rationalized that the blue wire was correct and prepared to flip the lever. It was begging to be flipped, but something in the back of her mind kept telling her it was wrong.

She stared at the tablet again, and then decided. She reached out and flipped the lever for the black wire that had no electricity flowing through it. When she did, the green light on the box dimmed and shut off.

She breathed a sigh of relief and immediately removed the laptop from the wires.

She thought back to simplicity again. The mind would naturally disregard the black wires while all of the other colors were there to draw your attention. As enticing as it would be for one of the brightly colored wires to be the savior, it was the black one in this case.

Donatella began making her way back to the stairs

leading to the lobby. Her pulse began to regulate when she wondered how BJ was faring over at the stadium.

Her reprieve was short lived when her phone rang. She thought back to the comment from Terri, "Let's just say communication in and out will be impossible." If that were true, her phone should not be ringing. A knot began to materialize within her core.

"Well, well, well. Special Agent Dabria, I wish I could say I'm surprised. With your back against the wall and with your dear friends in peril, you once again rise to the occasion and save them all. But to be fair, you had the easier of the two jobs. I mean it was a rudimentary bomb configuration that had only a slight twist. Unfortunately, I'm afraid you're protégé didn't fare as well as you did. I'm sure he will have nightmares and will likely need counseling from the screams that emanated from the stadium as he continued to fail time after time."

Donatella could feel the muscles in her jaw tighten, but she didn't have time to banter back and forth with Terri, "What is it that you want now?"

"All business and no fun, you are such the buzzkill. Alas, our match is currently a tie. One victory for me and one victory for you. But leaving our game in a tie is like kissing your cousin. Luckily, I planned for this. Who am I kidding, I stacked the deck for this to play out exactly as it did. You see," the menace dripping from her voice. "there is one more person who must succumb to my wrath before you and I have our final showdown."

Donatella evaluated the comment, pondering who she meant.

"According to my watch, if you hustle outside the courthouse, you'll be just in time to see the fireworks. When you're all done there, a package will be awaiting you at your home. I look forward to seeing you soon."

Terri disconnected the call, leaving Donatella standing alone in the basement with her phone in hand. The knot in her stomach tightened as she ran up the stairs in search of the exit. She knew that the prognosis was not good for whomever Terri had in her crosshairs.

25

"Hey, John. Congratulations," another well-wisher stated patting him on the back before shaking his hand. John smiled, exchanged a few memories, and then moved on. "Who was that?" Nancy asked as they made their way to the front near the raised platform.

"That was Charlie from the janitorial staff. He's been here at the Bureau for the last 15 years. On multiple occasions during my first month on the job, he let me into my office when I had left my key at home."

Nancy smiled, "Oh I'm sure he did. Geez, John. You would lose your head if it wasn't attached to your shoulders."

"Ha-ha. Very funny."

"Jokes aside, it seems like you know just about everyone who works in this building. It's clear that you're well-liked. Could it be my tough-and-rugged husband is a big old teddy bear at work?"

"Don't you go around spreading rumors. You can't ruin a man's reputation on his last day of work."

The married couple of nearly 35 years shared a hearty laugh enamored in the presence of each other.

Brewer craned his neck looking across the assembled agents. "I wonder where SSA Jessica Lawson is hiding. I figured she would be here since she will be assuming the helm. Although it's not a requirement for her to attend the retirement party, it would have been nice for her to meet with the agents in a social setting."

Brewer put the thought out of his mind as he engaged into a conversation with another well-wisher.

Two Hours Earlier

THE LONE FIGURE walked casually down the hall, headed for the stairway leading to the basement. There was no rush as the building, aside from the security guard on duty, was empty – for the moment. Bypassing the security guard was relatively easy because the lone figure worked in the building.

Years of training taught them that the easiest way to get caught when doing something you shouldn't is to act like you are doing something you shouldn't. So, the figure stopped at the security station and chatted with Carl the security guard on duty for a few minutes. They asked about Carl's family, his wife, Janet, and their newborn daughter, Lisa.

Carl was eager to share photos of Lisa asleep in the baby swing, presumably allowing him and Janet to get some rest as well. The figure didn't care too much for children, but appearances needed to be kept so they were all ears. After spending five minutes with Carl, the figure was on their way to the next destination.

If everything went as planned, a container would be situated in the basement, in a locked room that required special privileges to enter. To date, the figure's true employer had not let them down, and there was no reason to believe today would be any different.

The figure used the key card to gain access to the basement. While this was a security measure, the vast majority of the employees had access to the basement.

Nonetheless, one can never tell until the moment you are waiting for the access light to turn from red to green.

The figure's footfalls clicked with each contact to the concrete steps, a soothing sound to say the least. The figure mentally walked through the steps needed for the next stage of their assignment. Although they ran through the steps in numerous test cycles, this would be their first time executing in the real world. Realizing that the others involved in today's activities had already succeeded, the figure didn't want to be the one to fail. Furthermore, the figure had more riding on the success than anyone else involved.

The figure approached the room in question ready to use the badge for the first time to access this room. Although they had the right to enter the room, there were no reasons to set off any alarms prior to today's events. The figure tapped the security badge to the reader, and without hesitation, the green light appeared. *Time to get to work.*

The figure, also known as Jessica Lawson, had been groomed for this day for the last five years. The Bureau saw Lawson as an agent with the potential to run her own field office. Her intuition allowed her to maneuver through cases with startling efficiency. She was thoughtful in her dealings with other agents, suspects, and everyone she came into contact with throughout her career. She knew how to work the politics while keeping the respect of her peers. Her superior helped to fast-track her career ensuring that one day a field office would be hers.

While the Bureau was grooming her for upward growth, her handlers within The Syndicate were grooming her to take over the FBI.

The Syndicate had their eye on Lawson after narrowly avoiding her unearthing a plot they had to procure some rare stones from a black arts dealer. The operative they had in place to make the exchange was nearly apprehended. In the end, the operative escaped after a tip came in that the FBI was approaching the drop.

It took some digging, but they were able to secure the name of the FBI agent that led the raid. While it seemed unlikely that she would willingly join the organization, they knew if they applied the right amount of pressure, she would eventually see the light.

The powers to be within The Syndicate realized having someone highly placed within the FBI would open up doors they never imagined possible. So, it became imperative that she continue her rise within the Bureau as they proceeded to secure her services for their needs.

THE WOOING PROCESS, to their surprise, went much better than expected. On a warm summer day, Lawson arrived home to find a visitor casually sitting in the rocking chair on her porch. The vibe given off from the guest didn't signify a threat, nonetheless Lawson's antenna was up for the first sign of trouble.

"Can I help you?" Lawson inquired, hand swinging closely to her gun with each step she took.

"Ms. Jessica Lawson, I presume."

"Yes, that's right," she responded becoming wary of the guest, the swinging hand now hovering over her weapon.

"I have to say, it's nice to meet you. Don't worry, I won't take too much of your time. I'm here to offer you a job," the visitor said with a smile on his face.

"I already have job, so I think I will pass."

"Ah, but you haven't even heard what the job is yet. Trust me, it's something that I'm sure will interest you."

The guest pulled up an envelope that was sitting next to the arm of the rocking chair. "Why don't you take a look at the contents within the envelope. I'm sure you'll find it of some interest to you."

The visitor outstretched his arm with the envelope in hand. Curious, Lawson grabbed the package and pulled out the contents.

The color in her face drained when she pulled the contents from the package. She stared at documents and pictures, unable to comprehend how they had this information.

WHEN JESSICA WAS a high school student, she was responsible for the death of her best friend. The two were racing back from the local amusement park in separate vehicles. At various points their speeds surpassed 100 mph.

Being so young they believed that they were invincible.

Lawson, who was trailing her friend as the designated finish line approached, was competitive and didn't want to lose. She made the calculated decision to tap the back of her friend's bumper, not understanding the physics involved.

Jessica sped up just enough to have her left front bumper aligned with her friend's back right bumper. When she tapped the corner, the car began to spin out of control. As she bypassed her friend's vehicle it began to flip end-over-end in the middle of the highway, something Jessica saw in her rearview mirror.

She slammed on her breaks prepared to go back and help her friend when the car caught fire and was immediately engulfed in flames. She sat there, frozen, unsure what to do. She was 100 percent sure that her friend did not survive the inferno created by the flame and if she called the cops, they would have questions that she wasn't sure she wanted to answer. She saw her life flash before her eyes and decided she would take off.

Now, in her hand, she held a picture of the wreckage along with a police report that still showed the incident as a cold case.

She stared uncomprehendingly at the documents before demanding, "Who are you?!"

"The who is not important. The opportunity I'm here to offer you is. Why don't we go inside to chat in a more private setting? I'm sure you wouldn't want to discuss the contents and the opportunity out here in the public."

Jessica Lawson climbed the steps, opened the door, and invited the visitor into her house.

. . .

As she walked into the secure room, the encounter with the strange male visitor that took place several years prior was no longer at the forefront of her mind. A number of things had changed since that encounter, she had changed since the encounter. Other than the lapse in judgement from her youth, in regard to the accident, she had walked the straight and narrow.

Now, the competitive streak that was displayed during that deadly race became her underlying focus. She was more cunning in her day-to-day interactions, something drilled into her as she undertook her role with her new employer.

She looked around and after a few minutes she found the crate she was in search of with the initials 'TS' on the bottom corner. Inside, she found the materials she was looking for and immediately began the assembly.

45 minutes later she was back in the lobby, "You're not going to stay for the retirement party?" Carl asked.

"No, I just needed to drop something off, but I wish I could stay. I have a recital with my daughter that I cannot miss," she lied.

"I wish your daughter all the best. Maybe once you are settled in, you can bring her up to the job and I can do the same with my youngest."

"That would be nice. I'm sure she would like that. She is always looking for a new friend." The words flowed so easily from her mouth but in reality, she was thinking *you will not be here long enough to follow through on that request.*

Present

JESSICA LAWSON STOOD outside the office of Susan Yates and knocked on the door.

From the other side she heard, "Enter."

Upon opening the door, she was mildly surprised to see another visitor standing at the floor to ceiling windows with her boss. As she walked closer, she realized it was Veronica King. One of her assignments a couple of years prior was to pull data related to Veronica King and her family. She was also tasked with conducting a bit of surveillance to learn their habits and their secrets. If she recalled correctly, Veronica's husband was Kyle King. Idly, she wondered what ever happened to the cheating bastard.

"Is everything set?" Susan asked.

"Yes, everything is in place. Now we simply sit back and watch as the chips begin to fall."

Them and their damn veiled references, Veronica thought. Again, she considered asking for additional details, but she had a sinking feeling in her gut that she would find out soon enough.

AGENTS from all over the Charlotte field office made their way to the retirement party for SSA John Brewer. The assembled group mingled for the first 20 minutes but they were now settling in for the main event.

While retirements from the Bureau weren't anything new, retirement from the person in charge rarely happened. As such, when a retirement was on the horizon for someone of Brewer's magnitude, they made sure to have a good time. Part of that good time was a roast of the departing agent from his subordinates. For some, they were sharpening their metaphorical knives in anticipation of the moment. For others, having the opportunity to unwind was a welcomed distraction from their daily grind.

Secretly, Nancy was looking forward to the roasting as well. She knew the stress the job placed upon her husband, although he hid it well. She knew how much he cared about each of the agents under his watch. At times he talked about them as if they were his own children.

For John, being a mentor to the agents and tracking their growth was the part of his job that he enjoyed the most. Now, as he sat on the stage in front of those he mentored and those he personally took under his wing, she could feel him beaming with pride.

Nancy watched a well-groomed 30ish-year-old male agent walk to the stand. His sandy brown hair was worn longer than she would have liked, but it looked good on him. He was dressed in a severely tailored black suit with a diagonal striped black and burgundy necktie.

"Lamb to the slaughter," she heard a guy comment to the woman sitting next to him.

A few minutes later, she understood the comment. The agent was to first person sent up to roast John. It was clear the remaining speakers wanted to see how Brewer would respond. If he seemed to go with the flow and was at ease, they were prepared to go with their "A" material. If he gave that fatherly, disapproving look that they knew all too well, they would need to dial it back. Way back.

As it turned out, they had nothing to fear. John laughed at the jokes lobbed at him and was a good sport about it. Agent after agent made their way to the podium, the next one funnier than the one before.

According to the program, there was only one more roaster on the agenda before they would turn it over to the final guest speaker. Nancy, caught in the moment, began to tear up thinking about how far her husband had come and knowing that she would now have him all to herself.

They heard the sound before they felt the rumble. Most of the agents familiar with the sound of an explosion immediately grabbed their loved one and began to sprint for the door.

Brewer, too, was quick to respond. He grabbed Nancy by the hand, "Let's go," he said urgently, pulling her before the words finished leaving his lips. He was moving faster than she knew he could move and found it hard to keep up with his pace.

Second and third explosions were heard when a fissure began to climb up the wall. The light fixtures overhead began to disengage from the ceiling bulbs, popping as they did.

Brewer and Nancy were following in the wake of the agent who began the roast when the floor gave way from underneath him, and he disappeared before their eyes.

Brewer adjusted their route, "This way!" he said as more pockets began to materialize in the floor.

The fourth explosion sealed the fate of the remaining partygoers. The entire ceiling, along with the remaining two floors above them, came crashing down completing the stacked pancake with the floor. Death was instantaneously for the Brewers as their necks were broken from the impact of the ceiling collapsing on them.

DONATELLA EXPLODED out of the courthouse unsure what she would see when she emerged. She frantically checked her surroundings looking for any sign of Buckley's next move.

Once again, Terri was one step ahead of her and this time it held grave consequences. She suddenly heard an explosion coming from the heart of uptown. In that moment, she knew Terri's target.

She ran, arms pumping, lungs burning. Her mind told her, *you still have time*; however, her heart warned her, *you're already too late.*

She blocked out the competing judgements and instead focused on the fury emanating deep within her core. She should have seen this inevitable outcome; she should have prevented it.

A second, third, and fourth explosion could be heard in succession. The sound was deafening as she grew closer to the fireball climbing in the distance.

She conquered the last corner moving at top speed to witness black smoke billowing skyward. This was the first sign that her heart was correct and it tugged at her emotions as she ran harder. A building that was normally present in the landscape was ominously missing.

She wordlessly internalized a prayer and outwardly a tear began to materialize. She distantly heard the horn blaring from her left as she ran through the intersection.

The smoke previously in the background now gave glimpses of its origin. The normally smooth concrete structure of the building lay crumbled and tangled with its typically unseen metal skeleton.

Upon later reflection she would recall hearing the screams and pleas amidst the rubble, but in this moment, she could only hear her failure. She could feel her mind beginning to side with her heart as despair began to settle.

Fire trucks and EMS crews raced past her seeking the reason for the frantic calls.

Donatella knew the reason and she knew the arbiter of this heinous act.

Arriving at the scene of what was once a five-story building, she now saw smoke, rubble, ash, and destruction. Resigned to the fact she had failed those she swore to protect, her mind and heart agreed at last.

With one final look, her eyes took in the destruction, while her mind and heart became resolute in their agreement - *Terri Buckley would not live to see the sun rise another day*.

JESSICA, Veronica, and Susan stood silently at the window overlooking the city. Susan looked down at her watch, "Now, Ms. King, you'll witness the game of chess played out in real life."

The floor-to-ceiling windows that surrounded the office were bulletproof and heavily insulated. So much so that the sounds from across the street were muffled to a mere whisper inside the office. As such, when the first explosion ripped through the Panthers stadium, Veronica never heard a sound.

The only sign that something was amiss was the smoke rising from the stadium.

The smoke is what drew her attention just in time to see a section of the stadium drop out of sight.

Veronica, unsure of what she had just witnessed, blinked rapidly to clear her focus. She watched, nearly horrified as another section of the stadium dropped out of sight. Her eyes traced the movement as section after section of Bank of America stadium fell into ruins.

King's eyes shifted over to the two other woman who stood fixated on the scene playing out in front of them. It wasn't until the entire structure could no longer be seen that their eyes moved in unison to another fixed location in the horizon.

That simultaneous action told Veronica that the events were not over. She, too, turned back toward the window, blindly searching for what was next to come. A few minutes later she received her answer.

The explosions that rippled through the FBI building at 3700 Wicker St. was also silent behind the windows. However, moments after the explosions began eating away at the structure of the building another set of smoke began stretching toward the sky. Veronica who wasn't sure where she should be looking a few minutes prior, had no doubt where to cast her gaze.

She watched as what looked to be a five or six story building, it was hard to tell from their vantage point, began to stack floor by floor as it plunged to the ground. Unlike the stadium, the disappearance of this building took place in nearly the snap of a finger.

"Well done," Susan said turning to face Jessica Lawson. "I assume you have everything ready for the next phase of your assignment?"

"I do," the woman said in a semi-detached voice. "I will begin placing phone calls once I leave this building. It is certainly a dark day for the FBI."

"Good. You're dismissed. Keep me abreast of how the talks proceed."

The woman nodded, turned on her heels and made her way to the exit. Veronica stood motionless, still looking at the two distinct trails of smoke dissipating into the atmosphere. Had she heard the two of them correctly? Had they orchestrated an event that would affect the FBI?

She was snapped back to reality when she heard, "Checkmate."

26

When Donatella returned to the courthouse, the Thompsons and the Grandsons had been evacuated. Now, as she changed gears on her Kawasaki, the scenery flashed by in a mosaic of colors.

Her failure clouded her mind while her blood boiled just beneath the surface of her skin. Those she called peers, though she didn't socialize with them much, were no more. John Brewer, a father figure who helped her navigate her career, had been Terri's last target.

She switched gears again approaching speeds of 110 mph with revenge being the only thought she could push through the fog. Terri would finally have what she had been aiming for since the day she taunted Donatella a few weeks prior, a confrontation. A confrontation that would leave one of them incapacitated, unbreathing, and no longer for this world.

As if working on autopilot, she pulled up to 300 Calgary Way. She recalled Terri saying that she had left something for her, and there, affixed to her front door, was a large white envelope. She stopped the ZX 20 paces from the door, climbed off, and aimed her walking direction toward the door. She yanked the package from the door ripping the back in the progress.

Inside she found a single sheet of paper with the following message:

WELL, it looks like we have come full circle. The venomous words you spewed to Brewer about me. Talking behind my back as if I was nobody and both of you were so damn important.

You said you preferred to work alone; well, you now have no one else at the Bureau to work with, so your wish has been granted. I suggest you be more careful with your requests in the future as they may just come true.

Alas, it's time for you and me to settle things once and for all. It's time for me to prove to you, and everyone else who ever doubted me, that I'm better than you.

For us to get this show on the road, you're going to need my location. Meet me at the scene of our first case. Although there have been renovations since the last time we were there, the location is still the same. We can call it a home-coming of sorts. I'll be waiting.

UNDETERRED, Donatella input her security code into the digital keylock and walked into the house. She was well aware of the location Terri outlined. It was a place that she hadn't visited since the encounter. Focused on her own despair, she realized that she hadn't called BJ.

Standing next to the blue ocean breeze orchids in the

foyer, she felt them giving her strength to push forward. She stilled herself and dialed BJ's cell phone. BJ typically answered her calls on the first ring, if not the second; however, this time it rang four times before he picked up.

His voice was full of pain and self-loathing, "Donatella, I failed you. I failed them. So many people –" he began to choke up. "So many people... died."

"BJ, it's not your fault," she said in her most comforting voice. "You cannot control the actions of a psychopath."

"But you were counting on me, and I failed." He began to sob on the other end of the line.

"BJ, I need you to pull it together. We are not done."

He abruptly cut her off, "I'm done. Donatella, I'm done. I cannot do this anymore." "Damn it, BJ," she chided in her most terse voice. "If you give up on me now, she wins. If you give up me and we do not put an end to her wrath, all of those people in the stadium and the FBI building would have died without justice."

"FBI building?" he questioned. She realized that he had not heard the news. "Yes, the FBI building. While I was able to save the Thompsons and the Grandsons at the courthouse, Terri had another bomb planted at the FBI building. I was unable to save them."

In that moment BJ realized that Donatella had also experienced a tremendous loss, and her own failure. Yet, she was not giving up. If anything, her voice and tone revealed the urgency and determination that she felt. It was then that BJ pulled himself together, "What can I do to help?"

"Terri has decided the location of her final stand." She went on to relay the details of the note that was left for her.

"Donatella, you know it's a trap."

"Undoubtedly, and thus the reason I need you. She figures you will be of no use to me after today's events, so we will have the upper hand in that regard. While I prepare to engage her, I need for you to virtually scout the location. I'll orient the drone in the backyard."

SEVERAL YEARS AGO, the two began researching drones with long-range surveillance capabilities. After weeks of research, they realized a drone to fit their needs was not available on the market for your everyday consumer. BJ assured Donatella if they could locate a drone with the surveillance specs they desired, he could modify the drone to address their long-range needs.

They decided to go forward with the DJI Mavic 2 Zoom. The base had the majority of what they desired, and the rest would be modified by BJ and his engineering cohorts.

A month after the purchase, the modifications were complete. The drone was shipped to Donatella along with a second remote and instructions on its use. The initial trial was a success with BJ taking full control of the drone from his home location. A few more cameras were added to its chassis to aid in a 360-degree view of its surroundings while in flight.

Today, the trials would be put under the gun with a true crisis situation.

ONCE THE PLAN was ironed out, Donatella disconnected the call, grabbed BJ's modified gear, and proceeded to her final encounter with Terri Buckley.

27

The last rays of sunshine were dissipating in the horizon when Donatella appeared at the location of her first case with Terri. They were in search of Pablo Rodriguez, a womanizing gun smuggler who the Bureau had an interest in speaking with.

Rodriguez made a run for it when agents Dabria and Buckley knocked on the apartment door. They gave chase, Terri a little over eager, which caused her to fall through a carefully hidden hole in the roof. The fall resulted in both of her legs being broken, something that left her with a limp to this day.

Feeling her partner should be vindicated, Donatella took things into her own hands when apprehending Rodriguez. An apprehension that left him unconscious in a dark alley just behind the bar he had met Donatella at that night.

The multi-story rundown apartment complex, along with the other apartments from that day, had been replaced with a state-of-the-art complex that spanned the entire block.

Donatella recalled an article about the apartment buildings being demolished; however, she wasn't aware of what became of the location. A tingle in the back of her mind urged that this had The Syndicate's fingerprints all over it, and as BJ stated, it was certainly a trap.

The silence on the outside gave a vibe of hushed silence on the inside. In her left ear, her communication device came to life with BJ on the other end. "I've circled this massive complex a multitude times, and I have not seen anyone enter or exit. I'm going through all of the records I can find, but the details are sparse."

"Do a search within Global Insights Security. I have a feeling Veronica King supplied the security measures for this building."

"Will do. And Donatella, be careful."

She nodded her head, a gesture BJ could not see, and disconnected the call.

Without further hesitation, she thought, *this is for you mom and dad* and then walked through the inviting door of the complex that audibly locked when it closed behind her.

The interior of the building gave a damp feel from the prison gray concrete walls running down the corridor. The floors also concrete, appeared to be poured into on solid block undisturbed with evenly spaced lines. The air smelt of drying paint and, oddly enough, floral air freshener. The only high-tech item on display was a 65-inch flat screen Sony BRAVIA TV. Against the muted colors in the corridor, this electronic device felt out of place.

The TV suddenly sprung to life with an obnoxiously bright white background. Donatella, who still stood in the same spot from when she entered the room, expected an appearance from Terri at any moment. True to form, the white light gave way to a video image of Buckley.

Unlike the previous images she'd seen of Terri in the last year, in this video she was dressed in black from head to toe. A handgun could be seen from the utility belt wrapped around her waist. Additional items were strewn from her belt; however, the lightning and distance made it hard to make them out.

Her hair was pulled back in a bun, no doubt a weapon was holding it in place. Her torso was slightly out of proportion to her frame which told Donatella she was wearing a vest.

"Special Agent Dabria, I'm thrilled you could join us after the rough day you've had. I do trust the married couples are doing well. No worries, the rest of this day is not about them. It's about you and me."

Donatella looked around the room preparing herself for anything that may come her way. She also looked for any hidden doors tucked into the walls.

"Before we can get started, you'll need another warmup to kick off the second half of our game. I would hate for you to walk into our encounter cold and unprepared. For this set of warmup activities, you'll proceed through the maze that has been constructed within this building. In fact, the entire building is a maze.

On your right," a panel materialized as the covering rotated out of the way, "you will find a lever. Throughout this complex you will continue to see them. They will open the door of your choosing. As you make your way through the maze you will come to a series of crossroads. At each one you will pick either the door on your right or the door on your left.

At each decision point, one of two things will happen. One option is you will enjoy a leisurely walk to the other end of the room. No impediments will be in your way. You can call it a reprieve.

However, the second option will require you to make your way through the room by any means necessary. When you enter the room, the door will close and lock behind you. The only way for you to exit the room is to make your way to the other side and to use the lever to open the door."

Skepticism must have been written all over Donatella's face because Terri said, "I can promise you the options are as I have said. And to prove this to you along the way, tempered glass has replaced the drywall separating the room. You will have the opportunity to see what was in the other room that you did not select. At the end, and when you are sufficiently warm, you and I will dance."

"Terri, why don't you dispense with the theatrics and come face me right now." "Where is the fun in that? Furthermore, a lot of money has been poured into this maze and it's important that we have our rat run through it. Now, I'll do the honors and open the first door for you. See you soon."

A new pathway appeared once a section of the wall slid out of place. In her ear she heard BJ say, "I heard all of it. Also, you were correct, GIS installed the security system for this building. I should have the schematics in a few minutes."

Donatella didn't respond directly, she simply coughed into her hand. This was a signal to BJ that she heard his transmission loud and clear.

Through the door, the decor had a major upgrade. The dull, nearly sterile, concrete on full display in the previous room was now gone. Instead, the lighting dropped to 70 percent of its intensity while giving off a bluish hue. The pathway was littered with quarter-sized lights embedded in the ground directing the way down the path. The sound of a soothing waterfall rippled down the limestone visible off to the right. By all accounts the scene seduced you into a state of calm; however, Donatella knew it would be anything but.

She wearily traversed the illuminated path allowing her keen sense of hearing to block out the waterfall and focus on other sounds; she heard none. The path had a slight bend and around the corner she found her first decision point.

This wasn't made obvious with the appearance of two doors, as the wall remained flat. However, as in the previous room, a panel materialized from within the wall with a lever omnipresent. Donatella thought about it for a second.

Most right-handed people tend to go to their left when faced with a decision, whereas most left-handed people tend to go to their right. Psychologically, you tend to go in the direction of your least dominate hand as a defense mechanism because you're subconsciously willing to sacrifice your least dominate side if you had to make a decision.

Donatella thought back to all of her confrontations with Buckley and realized she was certainly right dominate. With this knowledge, logic dictated that Terri would lean more to her left. But the question she needed to answer, what was Terri trying to accomplish? Seeing that she was hell-bent on Donatella's destruction, that would be her focus. Defense would not be her focus, she would be on the offense. By all accounts this meant Donatella should pick the left; however,

Terri was always unpredictable so Donatella flipped the lever on the right.

The door panel on the right-hand side slid to the right leaving an opening through the otherwise solid wall. Stepping on the balls of her feet, she walked through the opening preparing to defend if necessary. In this instance, Donatella guessed correctly.

Entering the room, she saw no impediments in her way, only the door at the end.

She looked to her left where there, behind the tempered glass, she observed the obstacles that awaited her.

Running through random spots on the floor were circular saw blades. They ran roughly 15 yards back and forth at different intervals. At waist height, a series of javelin-type poles slid in and out of the walls. Finally, a gate dropped from the wall and began moving forward in the direction of the exit door. Donatella realized that the gate was there to force your forward motion, not allowing you to backtrack.

She filed this information away in her memory bank as a method of dealing with future obstacles. At the end of the room another lever sat motionless awaiting input from the rooms occupant. For a minute, she wondered if this lever swung left and right, similar to the one she used to enter this room. If that was the case, another decision was to be made.

Donatella thought, *how many times in a row would someone follow their tendencies before they switched it up for the sake of not being predictable?* Donatella felt she was delving in the mindset of Buckley as she pondered how the traps would be laid out.

Ultimately, she decided Buckley would not start off this twisted game with an empty room on back-to-back sides. So, this time she flipped the lever to the left and walked through the opening.

The door slid closed behind her and the semi-dark room came into full focus once the lights fully illuminated. Unlike the last room, this one was not empty. In fact, in the center of the room sat a single chair, and within that single chair sat a solitary man.

Similar to Buckley, she could see that the man was dressed in all black. However, unlike Buckley, his attire was a ninja-yoroi, a ninja outfit. Across his lap sat a katana with light from the blade reflecting from its brilliant shine.

Donatella, a student of several martial arts disciplines, would respect tradition and no guns would be used. Likewise, she figured a katana would be readily available for her. She looked around the room as the ninja in the chair sat unmoving. On the left wall, 10 paces in front of her, she saw what she was looking for. She walked to the wall, pulled the sword from its perch, unfastened her utility belt, and hung it on the wall where the sword had been seconds prior.

She walked back to the center of the room, where for the first time the man sitting in the chair raised his eyes to meet hers. Silently he stood, walked the chair over to the wall, walked back to the center, and bowed in her direction. Donatella returned the gesture, and then they took their positions.

Donatella sized her opponent up as quickly as time would allow. She was taller than him by roughly six inches, which of course meant she would have the reach over him. She could tell by the he walked that he was light on his feet which meant he was probably quick. An advantage for him.

Donatella was proficient in hand-to-hand combat, but she

rarely used a sword. She found that, with her height, wielding a weapon of its length meant it would take a longer time for the intended strike to reach home, even if it was only a few milliseconds. Again, advantage to him.

With the ceremonial bows complete, the foe was on her instantly. He used a two- handed grip to swing the katana in a diagonal arc aimed at Donatella's neck. She managed to maneuver her own weapon in time to defend the blow. The sound of the tamahagane steels clashing together reverberated through the room.

He wasted no time as he performed a reverse pivot bringing the sword toward her waist as he spun. Again, she managed to reposition her own sword in time to block the attack.

He released the double grip he had on the blade as he stood from his crouch and with a short jab of his open hand, he hit her in the solar plexus with his palm. The speed and impact were both unexpected and the blow startled Donatella, knocking her off of her feet. Not only was he quick, but he was also powerful.

Donatella knew she couldn't stay on the ground so as she was falling, she completed a full backward roll, springing back to her feet with her weapon once again on the defense.

That decision turned out to be a lifesaving decision because just as she moved the blade into the defensive location, the ping from the impact once again filled the room.

The speed and ferocity increased as the ninja slashed right-to-left, left-to-right, on a diagonal with some thrust mixed in between. Donatella barely managed to fend off each attack.

She realized from the start of this encounter, she had

been on the defense and she could not manage to hold him off if she didn't muster some offensive moves of her own. She searched for an opening, but with the barrage of attacks an opening was impossible to find.

Racking her memories as she defended the onslaught, she recalled momentum.

With her foe on the attack, she could use his nonstop action against him. When he raised the katana above his head, she dodged to the right instead of blocking the incoming blow. The slice of the blade brushed past her face missing contact by mere millimeters. However, the move gave her the desired effect.

Her attacker, expecting to make contact with her blade or her person, was thrown off balance. With that change in strategy, the balance of power in this battle shifted completely.

Donatella, now standing nearly back-to-back with her attacker, shifted the position of the katana in her hands. With speed and force, she thrust the blade past her left side piercing the steel into the back of her opponent. She could sense the blade tore through the cloth, skin, organs, skin, and cloth again.

Her attacker dropped to his knees, the tip of the blade protruding from his torso. She didn't know it at the moment but, as the blade passed through his body, she nicked a corner of his heart and her opponent was suffering from internal bleeding that would lead to his demise.

Realizing the battle had come to an end, she showed respect for her opponent with a simple bow. She then moved back to where her utility belt was hanging, fastened it around her waist, and proceeded to the door at the end of the room.

As she walked, BJ spoke through the comms, "Nice

finishing move," he said catching her attention. "I've managed to infiltrate the GIS security and I now have access to all of the internal camera feeds." The pep in his voice had returned and she thought, *maybe he will be able to put this day behind him.*

"I have some good news and some bad news. From what I can see, you only have two more decision points to complete prior to your interaction with Terri. The bad news, she lied to you, yet again, and I cannot see anything past the last room."

Donatella slowed her progress as she was sure Terri was watching her every move. She wanted to give off the appearance that she was pondering what to do next, where in reality she was letting BJ divulge what he discovered.

"Although she said each decision point had a clean path and a path you would need to fight through, the reality is, none of the paths, except for the first one is clear. At the first decision point, both rooms were empty. What you saw that looked like the other room was a video projected onto the glass."

Donatella had been so busy with the ninja that she hadn't looked to see if the other room on the right of her current location was empty. She glanced over to see an empty room; however, the information from BJ proved it was a projection.

He continued, "Behind the doors of your next decision point are two formidable options. On the left, the room expands to be wider than the other two you have already passed through. Within that room I see at minimum of six opponents waiting for you. They do not appear to have any weapons, but the number alone is something to be considered.

The size of the room on the right has expanded as well. I only see two figures, but it appears they are carrying firearms. From the room's configuration, you will certainly be at a disadvantage when you enter."

Donatella approached the lever and flipped the switch.

28

B efore entering the next room, Donatella made the decision that she would not hold back. The battle with the ninja took more time than she had expected, thus she was sapped of more energy. If the information from BJ was correct, and to be honest, why would she doubt it, she had two more encounters prior to her battle with Terri. Finishing these confrontations swiftly was at the top of her mind.

When she entered the room, the door once again slid in place behind her and locked. She looked around observing the enormity of the room. Unlike the previous encounter, she entered this room prepared to be on offense.

In her right hand she carried one of her Shinobi knives as she searched for the first set of combatants. Her search ended with the appearance of two burly men and a petite woman. She thought back to the instructions from BJ and slid the hilt of the knife forward. She could feel the additional blades extract from the base, ready for action.

With a sideways flick of the wrist the Shinobi knife flew horizontally through the air. As advertised, after roughly five feet the other two blades disengaged and began to free-flow on their own path. The main blade struck home, hitting the first burly man in the chest. The blade from the right side of the Shinobi base connected with the side of the neck of the petite woman. A spurt of blood burst from her neck at the impact and she fell to the ground.

The blade from the right side of the Shinobi base missed the mark of the other burly man; however, Donatella was quick to pull her SIG Sauer and fire three shots into his chest. She surveyed the room in search of the other three enemies. Moving with stealth from behind a stanchion, a man and a woman fired semi-automatic weapons that forced Donatella to dive for cover.

Shards of wood exploded around her as she contemplated her next steps. She thought, *continue to press the advantage*, counted to three and slid from cover. The first foe to pass her metal sights was a man who wore a tactical vest. He had spent all of his ammunition and rushed to reload. Donatella squeezed off two shots directed at the bridge of his nose. Confident they were going to hit home, she rolled back behind cover as another fusillade of shots rang out.

Five shots spent, 10 remaining, she thought as she waited for the assault to subside. Once it did, she moved from cover, and that was her mistake.

Before Donatella walked into the room, BJ advised her that there were at minimum six occupants. While she accounted for five of them; she never located the sixth.

When she spun from behind cover, the sixth member of

the opposing force hit her in the chest with a four by four. The impact stole the breath from her body and knocked her off of her feet. While she managed to keep ahold of the SIG Sauer from the initial impact, when she hit the ground, the pistol spilled from her hand, and slid across the floor.

Her eyes involuntarily filled with water as pain shot across her torso. She shook her head a couple of times to clear the cobwebs and blinked her eyes back into focus.

When she did, she saw a muscular 5-foot 8-inch man standing over her with a satisfied smirk.

While she willed her body to move, her limbs were refusing to cooperate. She shook her head once again at which point her assailant bent down and picked up her pistol. He checked to ensure a bullet was in the chamber and then spoke.

"I was so hoping you would've offered a challenge, but you'll meet the same fate as the others I have faced. When you arrive in hell, tell them Vince Monroe sent you."

He pointed the weapon between Donatella's eyes, smile widening, and pulled the trigger. The gun clicked but no explosion, no smell of gunpowder. The audible click snapped her back into reality, mind now clear. The smile on her attacker's face dropped into confusion as he turned the gun to inspect it. In that moment Donatella extracted her expandable baton, squeezed the handle twice, and it expanded to its full length.

She pushed herself to a seated position, gaining the attention of her attacker. With the baton firmly in hand, she swung at his exposed knee with all the power she could gather. The baton bounced off the exterior with a sickening thud. While his knee didn't completely buckle, the impact had the intended result.

The aforementioned Vince Monroe dropped the gun to cradle his knee. Donatella retrieved it, and promptly placed two shots into the side of his face.

The remaining female foe relaxed her assault figuring her compadre had the upper hand and was caught flatfooted with the change in direction of this battle. She began to heft the semi-automatic weapon, but it was too late. Donatella, who was once again in full control of her faculties, lined the sights on her forehead and squeezed.

The metallic clang of the weapon was followed by the thud of the woman hitting the ground. Donatella extracted the partially spent clip from her SIG Sauer and slammed home a fresh one in its place.

In her ear, BJ came over the comms, "Are you ok, Donatella? That was cutting it way too close." He knew she wouldn't answer, but he felt compelled to ask. "Anyway, this is your last decision point before the encounter with Terri. From everything I can see, the last two rooms seem to be identical. In both rooms there are a pair of female twins. They are sitting, waiting on your arrival." There wasn't much more he could say, so he only offered, "Good luck."

Donatella pulled herself together and made her way to the next lever. She took the right decision point for no reason other than to even out the lefts and rights she had previously made.

Upon entering the room, the lights dimmed. The room wasn't cast into complete darkness, but she found her eyes adjusting, straining for any source of light.

The twins that BJ had mentioned were silhouetted at the back of the room. Donatella wasn't able to make out much about the twins or the room they inhabited. She decided this didn't matter and pressed forward.

Special Agent Dabria stalked toward her prey calculating her plan of attack. As she did, the twins began separating. This changed Donatella's plan; however, it simplified the equation. If she could fight them one on one, this certainly made things easier.

Just then, the door from which she entered opened behind her. She took her eyes from the twins to determine the twist Terri was throwing her way. The light from the outer room shocked her eyes and it took her a moment to adjust once again. When she did, she realized it was the other set of twins. The door shut behind them as the intruders began to spread to the corners of the room.

Donatella realized they had her surrounded and now her plan was rapidly disintegrating. Four on one were not insurmountable odds, she had dealt with worse. But she grew tired of this game and only wanted to finish things with Terri Buckley, once and for all.

As if in a psychic connection, the four women began to charge Donatella without a word being uttered between them. Standing in the middle of the room she was a sitting duck, so she fixated on the woman at her northeast and began moving in her direction. The other three women would need to adjust their vector points giving Donatella a few seconds to deal with the first woman.

Undeterred, the woman in Donatella's proverbial crosshairs didn't hesitate and continued her forward motion. Their collision, an inevitable conclusion, was met with

Donatella performing a baseball slide underneath and past the woman. As she slid, she reached down to her side extracting the baton.

The woman surprised with the motion did a 360 degree turn and was met in the face with a fully extended baton across the bridge of her nose. This was followed up with a backhand strike to her exposed neck and she crumbled like a sack of potatoes.

With her left hand, Donatella reached for a Shinobi knife. Since the woman who was at her southeast was now directly in front of her, Donatella let the knife fly. She knew this wouldn't be a fatal strike, as she didn't have time to carefully aim, but it would certainly slow her opponent down.

This left the opposite twins that were originally on her left side when this ordeal first started. Although the woman who was at her north would be the closer of the two, Donatella directed her path to the woman who was initially behind her.

It appeared that the second set of twins that entered the door after Donatella had come prepared for the battle as the still-standing twin brandished a weapon of her own. In the semi-darkness she couldn't discern what the other woman was carrying, but to Donatella it didn't matter. She would need to dispose of her quickly so she could focus on the two that were presumably still in the fight. That is if the Shinobi she had thrown didn't kill the woman as she suspected it hadn't.

When Donatella was 10 feet from her next prey an unexpected light sparked from the stick. It was at that moment she realized that her foe was carrying a stun stick. Before Donatella could advert her gaze, the woman activated the flashlight attached to the stick momentarily blinding her. She instinctively dove diagonally to the ground in hopes of avoiding contact with the electric volt.

Donatella could hear the spark of the stick slide past her head as she came out of her roll. She hadn't gone into any sort of convulsion, so she figured her defensive measure had saved her for the time being. Her eyes were still dazzled with the unexpected stream of light, so she parried twice to the left and with blind calculation swung her baton in a backhand motion.

While the chances were 20/80 at best that she would connect with the woman, she whiffed on open air. She quickly ran the calculations in her head as she fought to regain her vision.

The twins that entered the door after her would now be in front of her. One would be injured from the knife she threw, while the other still had the stun stick. The remaining living twin, who originally occupied this room, would now be coming in from her left if she hadn't changed trajectories.

Donatella pulled out another Shinobi knife, slid the hilt forward and threw it blindly to her left. If her calculations were correct, at least one of the three projectiles would connect with the twin approaching from her left. Again, likely not enough to kill her, but should slow her forward momentum.

Her eyesight restored enough to see the woman with the stun stick preparing to jab her in the right side. Reflexively, she used her baton to swat away the attack just in time. This caused the woman to spin with her back now to Donatella.

Dropping her own baton, Agent Dabria took two swift steps toward the woman and grabbed her wrist. The woman, unsuspecting of this move, was unable to mount a defense. Donatella violently turned the woman's wrist back facing her body and pulled the stun stick into her chest. She felt the woman's body go limp as the electricity coursed through her body.

There were now two women out of the fight. One twin from each set. She now needed to focus on the other two. She felt more than she saw the motion coming from her left and instead of dropping the limp body she now held in her hands, she turned the woman to deflect whatever blow was coming her way.

A loud crunch was heard as the assailant hit her limp sister in the skull with Donatella's expandable baton. Donatella dropped the body, retaining control of the stun stick, and shoved the stick into the remaining twin who had blood pouring from her abdomen. She collapsed, falling on top of her sister confirming another foe out of this fight. This left only one remaining, at least that is what she thought.

She surveyed the room preparing for her next encounter when she noticed the last twin laying on the ground with sightless eyes. To her surprise, the blind throw of the Shinobi was hilt deep into the woman's neck. Before making her way to the end of the room, she went back to where the two twins lay and retrieved her baton, leaving the stun stick behind.

Donatella walked to the back of the room where the final panel materialized. This time, instead of a lever, a single button sat affixed to a box. She did a mental inventory of her gear and her condition. She was at about 85 percent from a health standpoint and she had plenty of accessories left for this battle with Buckley.

"Donatella, this is as far as I can go," BJ said in her comm.

"There are no additional cameras and I assume you will lose service once you enter. I'll be waiting for you when you're done. Now go kick her butt."

She turned, faced the camera and gave a simple nod. She then turned back, took a deep breath, and pushed the button.

29

Terri Buckley watched her former partner traverse the maze through closed-circuit television. She made no illusion that the obstacles she placed in Donatella's way would stop her, and that was not the point. Each speedbump was under Terri's thumb.

The ninja was the first one she recruited to play part in this game today. She sent him a picture of his wife in which she was framed in her car, outside of her office, in a riffle scope. Along with the picture she left a note, I can get to her at any time and there is nothing you can do to protect her. She followed up the initial communication with additional letters and the final one instructed him where he needed to be and when.

The ninja was told to put up a valiant fight. If he simply let his foe live, his wife would die. However, if he put up a good fight, his wife would live, even if he didn't.

Similar communications were sent to each person in the maze. Some would be spared from battle while others would certainly be in a struggle of life and death.

Her purpose in this endeavor was to gain insight into Donatella's fighting acumen. She planned to use the encounters with her recruits to look for any advantage she could use in their conflict to come.

The last battle with both sets of twins proved to be interesting, indeed. It was a last second decision to have the other set join in on the fun. Watching how Donatella dispensed of all four of them was nothing short of genius.

She could almost delve into the mind of her foe as she watched her dismantle the twins. Almost. She realized Donatella was going to be on the offensive. This would be the best way for her to control the pace of the fight, not to mention when you are in attack mode, you are rarely on the defensive.

But this was different. She took out a threat as quickly as possible, and then followed up with momentarily incapacitating the next before focusing on the third. Temporarily incapacitating an enemy so she could then focus on another one was something Terri had never thought of when it came to combat. She was full go, destruction to all. She would need to keep that in mind for battles in the future.

With the conclusion of the final decision point confrontation, it was now time for the main event. Terri activated the panel within the room and waited on Donatella to join her.

Terri could see Agent Dabria before Donatella could see her. Although she fought through four rooms of enemy combatants, she didn't look worse for the wear. Her spine was tingling with excitement and she could feel the rage building that she would use as her catalyst for this battle.

DONATELLA WALKED through the door expecting to be face-to-face with Buckley; however, she was greeted with a set of stairs leading below the surface. Undeterred, she cautiously walked down the stairs her eyes searching every corner as she did. When she reached the bottom, she caught her first glimpse of her long-term adversary.

This was the first time they were in the same location since the Cleveland Museum of Art incident. During that encounter, Terri used a special poison blend meant to slowly kill the special agent. The rage Donatella felt when she arrived at the destruction of the FBI field office rose back to the surface.

"Well, here we are at last," Buckley said with an uncharacteristic tone of sincerity. "It's been a fun few years, but I have grown tired of our back-and-forth conflict. It's a shame it has escalated to this, but alas, here we stand."

"This has not been fun at all, Buckley. You're a murderous psychopath –" "Donatella," she said interrupting, "Can we dispense with the name calling? I am what society has made me, nothing more, nothing less. And let's face it, you are part of the society that has made me this way. So don't stand on your soapbox casting stones at me. It's time you bear responsibility for this predicament we find ourselves in today."

"The only responsibility I bear is not ending your miserable existence the night we were at Aaron Smithville's house. I could have spared a whole lot of innocent people, a lot of pain and suffering."

"Wow, look how far you have come. Back then you would not hurt a fly, now you are ready to murder without a second thought."

Agent Dabria took another look around identifying several different exits out of this room; however, she didn't see any additional foes. She decided it was time to get started.

She began moving in the direction of Buckley's location and in response, Terri took the same measured steps backward. Warning signals flashed in her mind, *trap*, but she was determined to keep moving. At that moment she decided she could not afford to play on Terri's terms.

She pulled a Shinobi knife from her remaining stash and flung it in the direction Terri was walking. It wasn't meant to hit her, only to make her think on her feet, to react, and with that, the confrontation between Buckley and Donatella was underway.

Terri stopped as the throwing knife flew past her ear. The look in her eyes said she hadn't expected this and to Donatella it didn't matter. She picked up her speed, a walk into a jog and then a jog into a run. For Terri's part, she decided it was time. She reversed her direction and headed directly toward Donatella.

When the two were roughly 10 paces apart, she thought back to the conflicts she watched between Agent Dabria and her recruits. When she ran head on with a foe, she slid under the strike and attacked the woman from behind. Buckley decided she would be ready for this.

Donatella, for her part, realized if BJ was able to infiltrate the security cameras, Terri was probably watching. If that was the case, that gave Buckley some time to study her fighting techniques. She decided she would need to adjust on the fly.

If Terri expected her to slide past and attack her from behind, the best defense would be to side the slide and prepare to attack as she rose. So, Donatella decided she would also sidestep. In doing so, she would be standing right in front of Terri when they closed the distance between them.

Once the distance was closed, the scenario played out as Donatella expected. Terri stepped to her left, Donatella's right, and Donatella mirrored the move by stepping to her right. This left her directly in front of Terri where she struck her with an open palm under the chin.

With her momentum behind her, and the element of surprise on her side, Terri absorbed the full blow. The sheer power of the impact lifted her off of her feet and catapulted her backward. To her credit, Terri recovered quickly and before Donatella's follow up kick to her ribs could connect, Terri rolled to the side and bounced back to her feet.

Buckley countered the opening salvo with a kick aimed at her opponent's exposed right mid-section. Sensing the counter coming her way, Donatella tucked her side, shrinking the target, and absorbed the retaliatory blow. Terri, trying to press what little advantage she had, swept the legs from underneath the agent dropping her to the ground.

Through all of her training, Donatella was taught to stay off of the ground, and this training proved to be useful. When she hit the concrete floor, she rolled to her left, narrowly avoiding a knee from Buckley that was meant to connect with her chest. Both women stood to their full height after the initial clash. Collectively, without saying a word, this first round was deemed a draw. Terri, never one to stay still long, kicked off round two.

The former special agent knew she had the speed and quickness advantage over her former partner. As such, she pulled a combat knife from her utility belt and continued her attack.

Donatella, who didn't carry combat knives as part of her loadout, sidestepped the initial slash. Terri was on her with relentless aggression slashing at her face, abdomen and any exposed limb she could find. She continued to avoid the majority of them, but she was well aware that she couldn't keep this up for long.

She quickly pulled a throwing knife of her own, and after her latest dodge, looked to go on the offensive. With their close proximity, there was no need to have three blades flying across the room. So, Donatella took aim and let fly.

Terri, aware of how deadly her foe was with throwing knives, tried to dodge the incoming projectile. Even with her quickness, Buckley was nicked on the earlobe as the Shinobi knife continued on its path.

Agent Dabria didn't waste any time. With Terri on the defensive, Donatella raced toward her former partner, kicking the combat knife from her hand. Terry countered with a left punch to the jaw, barley making contact with Donatella's chin. The blow, a glancing one, had minimum impact but it was enough to allow Terri to counter, once again.

This time, with her right-hand free, Terri managed to place more power into her blow and connected with the agent's left temple.

Donatella could see the blow coming, but she was too slow to react. Not being able to dodge the incoming attack, she spun 180 degrees with its impact. With her back now facing her opponent, Donatella used her height and reach to her advantage.

She kicked her right leg back at a 45-degree angle connecting with Terri's shin. She turned around preparing to continue the confrontation; however, Terri had another trick up her sleeve. She pulled a three-inch diameter ball from her utility belt and tossed it on the ground. An audible pop could be heard and immediately a blue smoke began to rise from the wreckage.

Donatella, not quite psychologically healed from the poison mist Terri forced her to succumb to in their last encounter, immediately retracted. She began having flash-backs of her body lying on the ground searching for her next breath. In the present, she felt the tightness in her chest and the shortening of her breath. Upon seeing the smoke, she was worried that Terri had poisoned her once again.

However, after a few seconds the smoke disappeared and so had Terri. Donatella looked around the room realizing the former FBI agent was no longer present.

"BJ," she said into her comm. "Where did she go?" Silence.

"BJ," she said again with more urgency.

Again, all she heard was silence from the other end. She concluded that he was correct; he had no eyes or ears into this fight.

With a more critical eye she looked at the various exits in the room. She discarded the one that she entered through as Terri wanted this fight to continue. There were three more doors. Upon additional inspection she realized the one in the middle had a faint trail of the blue smoke circulating around it. *That door it is,* she thought as she pushed her way through.

Beyond the door's threshold sat 15 steps leading further underground. At the bottom of the stairs Donatella followed the path that grew further into darkness the more she proceeded to walk forward.

She needed to pull herself together. Her mom, her dad, the fans at Panthers stadium, her peers, Brewer, his wife. They were all counting on her to avenge their deaths, but the smoke bomb had her nearly hyperventilating and paralyzed with fear.

In the deep recesses of her mind, she knew that she was not invincible; however, she did everything possible to tilt the playing field to her advantage, and thus increasing her odds of success. So, she wondered, *how do I tilt this playing field?*

She heard a faint sound from ahead knowing it was an invitation and not a mere accident. Terri was too good to accidentally make a noise. She was being baited and she knew it.

Instead of taking the obvious route in the direction of the noise, Donatella looked for an alternative path. There was little doubt in her mind that Terri knew this battlefield forward and backward so in that she had the advantage. As long as Donatella continued to follow Terri's path it was playing into her plan. So, she decided to improvise.

She slipped off her shoes to lessen the sounds her footsteps would make. She then began a quick reconnaissance of her surroundings. She searched for locations that could provide her the upper hand. She knew Terri's impatience would get the best of her and she would come out to stalk her prey, and in that instance, she would become the hunted.

From what she could see, there wasn't much that would give her or Terri the advantage. She continued to maneuver her way through the corridor going the opposite direction from where Terri expected her to go. As she did, sounds of water became audible. Faint at first, but the more she walked forward, the more pronounced the sound became. Traveling an additional 50 yards, she found the source of the noise.

Running underneath the building was a stream. She quickly decided that stream would not be the correct word, because as she moved closer, it was clear that the water was deeper than a stream, much deeper. For as far as her eyes could see, right-to-left and in front of her, all she saw was the body of water. She pondered how she could use this location to her advantage when she heard a metallic click.

TERRI REALIZED as she swung her blade back and forth at the Special Agent that she would be lucky to make contact. She also realized; it would only be a matter of time before her former partner decided to go on the offensive. When the Shinobi knife came flying in her direction, she realized Donatella's offensive plan had begun.

With a burst of speed that she didn't expect from the agent, she kicked the combat knife from her hand. Reflexively, she swung with her left hand, barely making contact.

However, she intentionally put power into the right-hand blow that connected with the agent.

She was satisfied to see the blow spin the agent 180 degrees until she felt Donatella's foot connect with her shin. At that point she decided to move on to phase two of her plan.

She had numerous gadgets that she could use in the battle and the one she needed at this moment was a distraction. That distraction she decided would come in the form of a smoke bomb. She pulled the spherical device from her utility belt and slammed it against the ground.

She figured this simple childlike low-tech device would provide her the time she needed. She heard Donatella suffered from an acute case of PTSD. A result from the poisonous serum the agent endured at her hands. This meniscal device would render her useless long enough to perform her escape.

When the smoke began to rise, she could see her adversary's pupils expand to the size of saucers. While she wanted to revel in the sight, she needed to enact the next part of her plan.

She moved expertly to the middle door, retrieved another smaller spherical smoke bomb, and threw it to the ground. She figured once the first smoke bomb dissipated, the agent would be on the search for her. Subconsciously, the appearance of smoke at the middle door would entice her to follow through.

Once through the door, she proceeded down the stairs. It was at this point that she realized she had her greatest risk.

In her studies of Special Agent Dabria, and after watching the way she worked through her warmup in the building, she felt the agent liked to work in situations in which she controlled the parameters. It was true, she walked into unknown situations all the time, but once there she would do her best to turn the situation into her advantage.

It was with this thought that Terri Buckley took her biggest calculated assumption.

She activated the device some 80 yards away in the north. Once the agent reached a certain point in the sublevel, she would trigger an unseen device. That device would make a subtle, yet indistinguishable sound. A sound Buckley knew her foe would hear and a sound she hoped had the desired effect.

In the meantime, she would lay in wake waiting on the agent to make her appearance at the preordained location. She would only have a few minutes to ensure everything was set for Donatella's arrival, but she would be ready.

She heard the agent's footfalls on the stairs, *just in time*, she thought. She listened closely for the planted sound and after another minute she heard it. She envisioned Donatella processing what she heard and how she would deal with it.

It was taking the agent longer to react than she thought necessary and then it dawned on her. While she waited to hear the steps from the agent, she didn't think about the agent moving around in stockinged feet.

A surge of adrenaline coursed through her body as she realized the agent could be closer to her than she expected. *Smart move*, she thought as she moved to her next checkpoint. She wasn't sure how long it would take for the agent to appear at the manufactured lake because she didn't know exactly where she was in the underground setting. Nonetheless, when she arrived, Buckley would be prepared.

When Donatella arrived, Terri thought she saw the smug look of superiority on the agent's face. Little did the special agent know, this was a spot picked out by Buckley, for her advantage, and it was time to move forward with this confrontation.

For this special occasion, she procured a single-action Colt 45 revolver. She felt that she was overcharged for the gun, but in the end felt it would be worth it. She wanted the agent to hear the cylinder as it spun once she pulled back on the hammer. She wanted her to know what was coming and there was nothing she could do to stop it.

She lined up the barrel with Special Agent Dabria's left shoulder, pulled back on the hammer, reveling in the sound of the cylinder rotating, and squeezed the trigger.

30

Donatella felt the impact of the slug hitting her left shoulder as the sound from the shot assaulted her ears. The impact spun her three-quarters of the way around in a circle as she spilled onto the ground.

Her mind began to calculate where she went wrong. It didn't take long for her to process that she had once again been set up. This moment, this room was exactly where Terri wanted her to be.

As she lay there on the ground, she heard the distant sound of motors beginning to churn. For a moment she wondered if her ears were affected from the boom of the Colt firing. She continued to listen as another sound began to emerge.

The water, which sat peacefully in its manmade container, began to lap against the retaining wall next to her. What started as a splash in the beginning began to grow in intensity.

She next heard the smirk in Terri's steps as she approached from wherever she had been waiting. "Tisk, tisk,

Agent Dabria. Looks like you've gone and had yourself another accident. What is it, three times now that you have been shot in the same shoulder? I'm willing to bet the doctors would find it hard to repair the wound this time. But it doesn't matter, you won't live long enough for them to do anything about it."

Terri laughed inwardly as she could feel victory was close at hand. Yet she didn't want to rush this moment. She wanted to savor the feeling of finally besting the woman that the world thought could do no wrong.

She continued her approach, "You hear that?" she asked as the water's force continued to grow. "That, my dear Donatella, is the sound of your pending doom, your final resting place." Feeling full of herself in that moment, she couldn't help but to gloat.

"I designed this place, this maze if you will. Once you made it through your encounters with the group I assembled, you and I could officially battle. A battle in which I would best you at last. But then I thought, what to do with the body? I pondered this for a while and decided to alter the design."

Her lips involuntarily curled as she recalled the memory. "A watery grave would be fitting for someone of your stature. Once I ended your wretched, despicable existence, the raging waters would carry your body out into the middle of the Catawba River. And there, you would rest for all of eternity."

She arrived at the agent, staring down at her prostrate body with a smile plastered across her face. She was prepared to finish her lengthy monologue when she realized something was wrong, something was missing.

The Kevlar t-shirt that BJ sent as part of his weapons upgrade performed as advertised and while the bullet spun

Donatella around to the ground, the five ultra-thin layers, two of which were Kevlar gel, stopped the bullet's penetration.

Donatella, thinking quickly on her feet, realized Terri would come in close to voice her triumph figuring the upper hand was all hers. Unfortunately for her, victory would not be the case.

Special Agent Dabria kicked at the inside of Terri's knee, connecting with less force than she had planned. Nonetheless, it did the job of crumpling the woman to the ground. She could hear the water's relentless rage as she rose to her feet. Standing fully erect, Donatella kicked her opponent in the ribs, flipping her over a couple of times from the impact.

The vest that Terri wore absorbed some of the blow, but it didn't matter. Fueled by her pent-up anger, Donatella pulled her up by her hair chopping her once in the throat. She didn't want her to utter a word and was satisfied as Terri gasped for air.

She thought back to Bree and the fact that she was now in counseling because of the nightmares from nearly being blown up. Donatella connected a right hook to Terri's face. She flashed back to her car flipping over, and over, and over on I-77 as she chased down the henchmen who abducted Jasmyn and her unborn child, another hook, this time a left.

The backdrop of the raging water propelled her. Donatella flashed back to the men, women, and children whose only flaw for this day was attending the home opener at Panthers stadium. With as much strength as she could muster, she planted another right hook into the other woman's jaw. She was becoming lost in the moment, but still in control.

She thought about all of her colleagues and Brewer. The

indescribable pain they must have felt as the FBI field office collapsed on top of them, another left hook to the face. Buckley, weakly tried to counter, but Donatella shooed away her attempt.

She thought back to the video Buckley had the audacity to play of her parents last moment on earth, another right hook. She thought back to the video of her mother singing her happy birthday, and the wish young Donatella made to let that perfect minute last forever. With a surge of energy, Donatella Dabria let out a primordial yell and kicked Terri in the midsection flipping her several times into the retaining wall of the now raging water.

Terri tried to stand but Donatella kicked her in the ribs again, this time hearing multiple snaps. She pulled the woman up, this time by her vest.

"You do not deserve to live," she said in a detached voice that made her sound inhuman. The two women, former partners, now sworn enemies, locked eyes. Defiance could be seen in Terri's as the life was slowly draining from them.

Terri said in a raspy voice affected by the chop to the throat, "An angel of death you are indeed. We'll pick this up in hell."

Donatella looked her in the eyes and responded "No, we won't." She lifted Terri by her vest and tossed her over the four-foot retaining wall. She watched as the artificial current swept her along, pulling her under the surface once, twice. On the third, she went under and didn't resurface.

31

W hen the doorbell rang, Jasmyn Thompson had the sinking feeling in her gut that it was the bad news that they had been dreading.

The newlyweds, Sal and Jane Grandson, joined the Thompsons back at their home in Driftwood Springs. Before leaving the courthouse, they spotted the motorcycle belonging to Special Agent Donatella Dabria amongst their vehicles. However, the special agent was nowhere to be found.

When they arrived back at the residence, they heard the news of the FBI building collapsing to the ground. Speculation from the group ran rampant until they decided on the most logical thought.

Donatella, with plans to attend to the wedding, had been called into the FBI building and while she was there the building collapsed. They argued over why her motorcycle was still at the courthouse and they couldn't come up with solid reasoning.

Jasmyn tried her phone for the next few hours, falling

deeper into despair with each unanswered call. Marcellous tried to find the words to comfort his wife, as he too was dealing with the apparent loss of a friend, their baby's godmother.

For their part in the discussion, the Grandsons tried to put a positive spin on things. "You can never count her out," Sal countered. "We have witnessed first-hand how she perseveres against insurmountable odds. Let's not give up on her yet." But even as Sal continued to give hope, his spirits were dampening as each hour passed.

So, when the doorbell rang at 1812 Garden St., Jasmyn and the collective group, prepared for the worst. With eyes swollen and nose puffy she opened the door and screamed out in disbelief, "Oh my God!"

Marcellous, hearing what sounded like distress from his wife, was first to react. He sprung from the couch, running toward the door with Sal hot on his heels. He turned the corner in time to see a woman, in completely black attire, fall into his wife's arms.

"Donatella, oh my God. Are you ok?" Jasmyn asked catching the woman from hitting the marble floor. Her nursing instincts kicked into full gear. "Marcellous, go and grab my medical kit. Sal, go to the suite and grab towels from the linen closet. Jane, help me get her to the couch."

Without question, everyone sprang into action. Jasmyn and Jane helped Donatella lay back on the couch.

"I'm, I'm fine," came the hushed words from the agent. "Some water if you –" "You are not fine!" Jasmyn fired back. "People who are fine don't collapse into the arms of their friend. People who are fine do not appear in tattered," she stumbled looking for the right words, "battle gear. People who are fine do not scare the people that care about them. The people who think they will never see them again. So, no, you are not fine."

Sal was first to arrive. He sat the towels next to Jasmyn while Marcellous opened the kit and handed it to his wife.

For the next 20 minutes Jasmyn expertly tended to Donatella. Everyone watched wordlessly until she said she was all done. "Now, where on earth have you been? We've been worried sick about you. When we heard what happened at the FBI office we thought," the words caught in her throat. "We thought we lost you."

Donatella thought for a moment on how much she would share with the assembled group. Then she decided to level with them.

She talked through tracking Terri to the abandoned warehouse. She walked through the carnage that took place at the football stadium that BJ tried to prevent, but ultimately failed. She hesitated on telling them how close she came to losing them all at the courthouse, but ultimately decided to tell that as well.

When she arrived at the discussion about the FBI building, her jaw involuntarily tensed. She never had an opportunity to save them, none at all.

Jasmyn, Marcellous, Jane, and Sal listened to each word that came from the hoarse voice of the special agent, never once interrupting.

"Going into the confrontation with Buckley, it was clear that she was working an angle and that it was a trap. Nonetheless, after the annihilation that took place by her hands, trap or not, I had to go face her. She made it clear, only one of

us was leaving there alive, and I was fine with those stakes."
Jasmyn raised an eyebrow.

Sal asked, "So is it over? Is she finally gone?"

"Yes," she said with intensity blazing through her eyes,
"It's over."

The room was cast into silence at the implications. The
woman who terrorized them, and countless others in the city,
was now dead at the hands of Special Agent Dabria.

Marcellous, looking to break the tension, asked, "Who
wants pizza?"

———

VERONICA KING ADDED the final touches on her grilled
salmon and risotto dinner. She asked a friend to watch Gina
for the evening. With everything she witnessed today, the
destruction of Panthers stadium, the destruction of the Charlotte FBI field office, the death of countless innocent people,
she couldn't have Gina around tonight. She wrestled with the
fact that The Syndicate, a criminal organization that she was
now associated with, could murder so many people. Not only
had they murdered those people, but they also saw it as a
game.

Then the realization that the woman, the head of the
organization, was the aunt of Special Agent Dabria was
something she would have never guessed. With this knowledge, the resemblance was right there in front of her. She
didn't know how she could use this information, and better
yet, should she use this information. This organization was
not one to be toyed with and even the thought of using this
information sent chills down her spine.

She finished assembling her plate, poured her third glass of wine, and walked her dinner to the table. She said her grace and took a bite of the risotto. As she chewed, she lamented the thing that bothered her the most.

After witnessing the murderous mayhem this organization could unleash, she wasn't shying away. While she was shocked at the events of the day, she wasn't appalled, and a part of her felt that she should be. Instead, she felt more drawn to them. She could feel the power radiating from the decisions they were making.

She took a bite of salmon followed by a sip of wine and contemplated one question.

How far am I willing to go? She was already involved in the murder of her husband and his mistress, but she was not the one who ultimately dealt the final blow. Could she take a life, that of someone she cared for and was special to her? She could never bring harm to Gina, for she was the person she loved most in the world. There was always... she stopped in mid-thought when the doorbell chimed.

She wasn't expecting any company, so her mind jumped to the worst-case scenario, *something happened to Gina.* Then again, she would have been called if that were true.

She dabbed the corners of her mouth with her napkin, folded it in half, and sat it next to her plate. Casually, she walked to the door pondering who could be stopping by unannounced. Upon opening the door, she had her answer.

Slouched against the door jamb battered, bruised, with her clothing plastered to her skin was Terri Buckley. The distinctive features that made up her face were now melded into an assortment of cuts, bruises and full surface swelling.

"Jesus! What happened? Are you ok?"

"No." Was the only words spoken as she limped across the room in search of a place to sit.

"Let me, let me go get something," was all she could muster. Veronica King hurried off in the direction of the bathroom, and then slowed her pace. She had a travel-sized first aid kit in the spare bathroom downstairs, but that would not do. Not in this situation.

"Let me run upstairs," she said with her voice disappearing as she climbed the flights. She didn't have any training in this but figured it couldn't be too hard. She'd seen it done several times on the TV shows that she watched. She could call someone, but she figured she'd better do this herself.

She walked into the bathroom off of the owner's suite, opened the door to her vanity and found the kit she was looking for. With haste, she made her may back through her bedroom, and down the stairs.

When she arrived, she stared at the woman sitting in her chair. Her face was so grotesquely swollen that she couldn't decipher if she had fallen asleep or if her eyes were open.

Terri, who found sitting in the chair to be uncomfortable, tried to think how it all went so wrong. Donatella bested her at her own game, something she could hardly believe. To make matters worse, she had been the one thrown into the water. She recalled the currents pulling her under, several times. She tried to fight the waves, but it was futile. She ensured that, when she designed it.

In her mind, she knew that once she hit the water, she was dead. When she went under for the third time she blacked out, until she awoke floating in the middle of the river. She could hardly believe her fortunes, something she would not take for granted.

Her thought process was broken when she heard an all too familiar sound. She strained to open her eyes and to clear her focus. When she did, she found herself at the other end of a cocked and loaded 9mm handgun. She heard Veronica say, "It's nothing personal, but I plan to be queen one day, and in this game, you are the pawn."

The last thing she heard before her world went dark was the explosion from the barrel of the gun once the trigger was pulled.

WITH THE CONFLICT between Terri Buckley now at an end, Donatella has a new enemy on the horizon. An enemy who has infiltrated the FBI. Pre-order **Treacherous Deceit** and witness how this next chapter unfolds.

Scan to pre-order Treacherous Deceit

IF YOU ENJOYED "ANNIHILATION", the conclusion of the Terri Buckley Saga, please consider leaving a **review** so that other readers just like you can locate this novel.

Scan to review Annihilation

Note from the Author

THANK you for your purchase of "Annihilation", the third book of the Donatella Series. In writing this novel, it was time for the conflict between Donatella and Terri to come to an end. The key question that played in my mind for months while writing this novel was, "Should Terri be killed off?" I honestly went back and forth on this question because writing Buckley's character took on a life of its own. However, it allowed a new batch of antagonists to step into the lime-light. And now we have a nice cast to select from.

Susan Yates – the reveal of Donatella's aunt being the head of The Syndicate leaves several paths for this storyline to take on. Especially, what was it about this job that made her orphan her niece while killing off her own sister?

Veronica King has continuously grown in her own path over the last two novels. She now knows a secret many people don't know; Susan is Donatella's aunt. Is this something she can use to her advantage in the future, or will this be her own undoing?

Jessica Lawson will be taking over the helm of the FBI field office after its destruction at her own hands. Being a member of The Syndicate, and now the boss of Donatella, we are just at the beginning of her tale.

I'm excited about where the series is headed and I look forward to taking you on the journey with me. If you'd like to stay connected to the Donatella Series, sign up for my **newsletter** and be alerted on the new discoveries within the Donatella universe.

Sincerely,

Demetrius Jackson

SPEAKING OF THE DONATELLA UNIVERSE, I'm excited to announce a new series that will be kicking off soon. Detective Carl Sampson, from "Hour of Reckoning", will be leading off the first book of the new series. The first book, Pseudonym, will be the next book released. Enjoy the excerpt below:

Pseudonym Excerpt

The voice that reverberated was silently loud because, after all, the voice was in his head. This voice, a recently consistent voice, had never failed him in the past. It was a voice that aided him in times of fight or flight decisions; however, as of late its fight was much more resilient than its flight. Today, the voice was telling him that there was no reason for her to live. It had already been scripted and it was time for her to play her part. It would be a glorious cherry on the top of a well-crafted tale.

He flipped the mental coin in his head. This was his rational side. This side, the one that many consider the angel on their shoulder, could be counted on when he was faced with moral decisions. He liked this side. It had served him well throughout his life. He had never been in trouble with the law. Married a beautiful, wealthy woman who loved him dearly. It provided sanity in his life. He could always count on this side to walk the straight and narrow.

However, when this side, the rational side, spoke today, it was slightly jarring. "She's already seen you, and she's already here. Might as well finish what she was brought here for and plan better next time."

For a moment, he was frozen into shock. He mentally flipped the coin two more times. "Cherry on top" was the first response. "Finish and plan better next time" was the second.

Both palms were saturated with perspiration and shaking with the anticipation of what was to come next. He knew what was to come next as he researched it from every angle and, after all, he had already written it. He knew Dillion's hands would not be wet, nor would they be shaking. They would be as steady as a surgeon's hands before a triple bypass surgery. He had breathed life into Dillion to have ice water coursing through his veins and it was time for his to do the same. Yet, when he tapped into the sensors in his body, he simply felt the warm plasma pumping from his heart to the furthest reaches of his limbs. He'd have to work on that.

The time for deliberation had come to an end. He stood up, walked to the door and turned the handle. Before entering he could hear - feel the muffled cries for help. This gave him a sense of pride. The muffle had been correctly anticipated as it had been written, as it had been scripted. He wondered before pulling the door open, would she have the wide, pleading, hopeless eyes that Dillion saw when he entered the room? "Only one way to find out."

He opened the door, and there across the room, bound to the bed lay the woman of the hour. The single light that shone a triangular pattern across the room barely kissed the edge of the bed illuminating her left side. He approached, footsteps echoing in the chamber. With each step he could feel her anguish as the muffled sounds grew more urgent.

Now, standing at the edge of the bed, the answer to his previous question was answered. The eyes were indeed wide, and pleading, but he didn't sense the hopelessness. Maybe she thought there was some bargaining chip she had that would save her life. She was attractive, and he had seen her on several occasions work her charms to get exactly what she wanted. But little did she know, that's one of the main reasons why she lay strapped to this bed.

She was not selected at random. She was selected because she was a treacherous slut who used her good looks to barter her way through life. Dillion would not have stood for this and neither would he.

He thought two out of three wasn't bad. If he were in an academic setting, that would be a failure; however, if it were a field goal percentage in basketball, he'd be a superstar.

Nonetheless, he needed to figure how to elicit hopelessness for the next time. He knew there would be a next time because the moment he stepped through the door and heard the increasing muffled cries, a sense of satisfaction went pulsating through his body.

He looked down at her, mouth gagged, makeup running, eyes locked on his. He pulled the scalpel from his smock and said, "Hello, Mandy. "Let's get started my dear."

PRE-ORDER **PSEUDONYM** TODAY!

Scan to pre-order Pseudonym

Annihilation

First edition: April 2021

ISBN 978-0-9771133-5-4 (paperback)

❀ Created with Vellum